JONATHAN CARTER grew up in the London sub-urbs with a psychic grandmother and an elkhound called Magnus. As a child actor he appeared in television advertisements and, in his late teens, played rock guitar with members of Shriekback and the Associates. He also pursued his interest in art, winning the Jeffrey Archer Prize in 1988 in the Southbank's Spirit of London competition. Later, as a film journalist, he worked for various magazines and occasionally featured on BBC radio before becoming a full-time content producer for the BBC. During this time he began to write fiction, contributing to two books published by Faber and Faber (*Shouting at the Telly* and *Ten Bad Dates with De Niro*) and several literary publications. This is his first novel.

THE DEATH
OF
MR PUNCH

THE DEATH
OF
MR PUNCH

JONATHAN CARTER

PETER OWEN
London and Chicago

PETER OWEN PUBLISHERS
81 Ridge Road, London N8 9NP

Peter Owen books are distributed in the USA and Canada by
Independent Publishers Group/Trafalgar Square
814 North Franklin Street, Chicago, IL 60610, USA

First published in Great Britain 2016
by Peter Owen Publishers

PAPERBACK ISBN 978-0-7206-1885-3
EPUB ISBN 978-0-7206-1905-8
MOBIPOCKET ISBN 978-0-7206-1906-5
PDF ISBN 978-0-7206-1907-2

A catalogue record for this book is available from the British Library.

Typeset by Octavo Smith Publishing Services

Printed by CPI Group (UK) Ltd, Croydon, CR0 4YY

For Daphne and Leonard, wherever they may be

ACKNOWLEDGEMENTS

It's been a lonely task writing this book, but one that's been made possible – and slightly less solitary – by the support of Samantha Glynne, whose re-readings of Mr Punch's various incarnations have been invaluable. My two sons, Ari and Fred Carter, also deserve credit. Watching Fred become an adult has been a real inspiration, as has the never-ending curiosity of the indefatigable Ari. Thanks also to my brother Tim Nevil, whose stories spurred me on, and to Mike Veitch and Matt Cole for their encouragement. I'm also grateful to Dan Gosland, for guiding me through officialdom, and everyone at Peter Owen for their hard work and support – especially Antonia Owen, for her belief in the book from the outset. Finally, my heartfelt thanks go to Jan Roberts, without whom you would not be reading this. Jan – Nelly and I can't thank you enough.

1

A HOUSE IS NOT A HOME

He rubbed his eyes and peered into the gloom. All he could see now was the crude sketch of a room. Sideboard, bed, bookshelves, chairs, the usual roll-call required for so-called civilized living. He'd been woken by a bang, like the slamming of a door. More of a thump perhaps – his ears were not what they once were. At first he'd thought that there was someone in the room. But then he heard it again, and he was sure that it was coming from downstairs. He was relieved. But only a little.

The room felt colder than before, despite the fact that it was dawn outside. He knew this because he could see the sunlight burning the edges of the curtains, the leaden drapes that he'd been so careful to close before settling down for what was meant to be a nap. They'd made the usual scraping sound as he'd crouched below the window and dragged them along the old rail. They were always heavier than he thought they would be.

Now, though, he wanted to open them again and bring some light into the room, for all the good it would do. But he didn't dare. He was being watched. It would be like setting up a Tannoy and flying a flag from the roof. Instead, he reluctantly reached out towards a table lamp beside him, its silhouette barely visible, and pressed what he thought was a switch at the base of the lamp. But no light appeared. He was still only half awake, and his muscles were reluctant to cooperate. Even reaching out towards the lamp felt uncomfortable. That would teach him to fall asleep in a high-backed chair.

The bangs and/or thumps were getting louder now. Surely it was only a matter of time before whatever was downstairs began making its way upstairs.

He shut his eyes again. 'Stay calm,' he whispered to himself. 'Don't panic.' He took a deep breath. He had no choice – he had to take action. He donned the striped silken cap that he'd placed on the chair arm before his so-called nap and half-heartedly hauled himself up into the shadows. His yellow satin tunic, cold to the touch, made a slithering sound as he moved, its brass buttons glinting like fireflies as they caught the weak light from the window. Once upon a time he would have been able to find his way around this room blindfold. Now, though, as he stumbled through the darkness, it all seemed very unfamiliar.

Slowly he made his way towards the corner of the room. If he was going to see off intruders then he'd need a weapon. Alas, his slapstick was not to hand, so his walking-stick would have to do. It wasn't perfect, but it would do the job.

As he took the stick and held it in his trembling hand he could feel his spirits lifting. Or at least being brought to the boil. The small silver bell on the top of his striped cap even tinkled for a moment, and he suddenly felt like doing a little dance, albeit an arthritic one. Instead, he opted for a series of sweeping gestures as if in salutation, bowing and tucking one hand into his stomach while raising the walking-stick to the ceiling with the other. He paused for a moment in this odd pose. He was finding it difficult to straighten up. Reality, in the grim form of lumbago, had yet again elbowed its way into a glorious moment of fantasy. His back was getting worse. These days his profile looked more like a question mark than an exclamation, and it seemed to be getting more and more exaggerated, as if he were gradually being forced to forsake the sky and stare down at the dust.

Having eased himself out of his lavish pose he stood there in the half-dark for what seemed like minutes. The momentary burst of confrontational enthusiasm had gone now, and he could feel his fake fighting spirit leaking out of his fur-lined boots. Even the walking-stick was starting to feel heavy.

At least the room appeared to be getting lighter. The photographs on the sideboard were visible now, lined up like dusty windows on to better times. One of them featured a wedding. There he was, done up to the nines with his outsized smile; beside him was his beloved Judy in her green embroidered dress with its billowing skirt, her frilly bonnet framing her fulsome face. The happy couple were flanked by their brides-maids – or should that be bridesdogs? – dressed in dungarees. Burt and Hal, bull terriers both.

Despite the light, he was now beginning to wilt. It was starting to feel as if the air was gradually being sucked out of the room. He needed to sit down. All he could see now was Judy's face. The face he loved so much.

She'd left him in this very room a long, long time ago.

Last night, as he climbed the stairs, he was sure he could hear her voice. She was calling for him. 'Is that really you, Judy?' he whispered as he clutched the balustrade. 'Oh, please be there . . .' When he reached the landing he could see that the door was ajar. 'Hello, darling,' he said quietly as he entered the room and slowly made his way towards the bed. 'It's me. I'm back. I'm sorry it took so long, Judy. I think I remembered everything . . .'

The bed was empty, of course, and for a while he stood there in the gloom, the clock ticking relentlessly beside him, marking time with what sounded like a tiny shovel digging down, down into the earth. He stared at the pillow where she once placed her head. 'I thought you were here, Judy,' he whispered. 'Where did you go?'

He'd never forgotten the day she died. That overwhelming sense of hopelessness as her life force ebbed away, when she'd lain there in her white bed gown and nightcap, barely conscious. He'd put his face close to hers.

'Can you hear the singing?' she asked, smiling faintly.

'Yes, my love, I can . . .'

'They're calling me,' said Judy, slowly closing her eyes. 'I'll have to go to sleep now . . .' The words withered on her lips.

'Sweet dreams, my darling girl,' he'd whispered, barely able to speak as he tried to stem the sudden choking in his throat. She still looked beautiful, despite life's scars and bruises, and he felt honoured to have looked upon her for so long.

Devastated, he'd sat beside the bed in the old high-backed chair for what seemed like hours, with only the soft tick-tock of the battery-powered clock stopping the silence from swallowing him up. What would he do without her? She'd been around for longer than he dared remember. How would he be able to keep his brain from bursting without being able to tell her everything that came into his head? It felt like he would barely be able to put one foot in front of the other.

For a while he convinced himself that she was only sleeping. 'Sleep . . .' he said to himself. 'She said she was going to sleep. Which means she'll wake up again soon.' He was good at keeping ludicrous hopes alive, but this one was too far-fetched even for him. She was gone, and he knew it. His beloved Judy had begun the sleep of angels.

His memories were all he had now. Each one, however small, would be a victory against the tyranny of the present. It was the only way he was going to get through.

Suddenly there was a loud thump – more of a bang, perhaps – his ears were not what they once were. It sounded like the front door closing. They'd finally found him. He knew it. He tightened his grip on the walking-stick and made a fist with his other hand. In his current state this was less an act of aggression and more a way of redirecting the emotions that were threatening to overwhelm him. But it would fit the bill.

He could hear someone making their way up the stairs now, slowly and deliberately, trying not to make any noise. He had to hide. But where? The bell on his cap made a tinkling sound as he looked around frantically. In a sudden bout of irritation he snatched it from his head and was about to throw it across the room when it dawned on him that such an impetuous gesture would only make more noise. So he carefully folded it up and placed it as quietly as he could in his pocket.

Like a frightened child, he now crouched down beside the sideboard. The wall felt cold against his thin red silken trousers as he pressed himself awkwardly into the small space, brandishing the walking-stick before him like a pike. It was all he had against the world.

He closed his eyes and wished that he was somewhere else. He could see Judy's smiling face before him, and for a while he felt comforted . . . until her smile began to curdle. In desperation, he opened his eyes, but it made no difference. The face was still there, dangling in the darkness and decomposing right in front of him.

He watched with horror as one of her eyes began to bulge before slowly slipping down her cheek, while the other eye looked skywards. Her sturdy nose, meanwhile, was becoming splayed as if crushed. Worst of all, though, was her mouth. Once plump and full, it was now thin and lipless, populated with tiny yellow teeth like an old broken zip. He could see it moving. It looked like it was trying to speak.

Still clutching the walking-stick he tried covering his ears. 'No,' he said tearfully. 'Please, no.' But his pale protest didn't stop the words from creeping out into the darkness.

In desperation he began singing to himself. 'Be it ever so humble, there's no place like home . . . Be it ever so humble, there's no place like home . . .' He repeated the refrain over and over.

Suddenly there was a bang on the door. Judy's dying face disappeared along with its ghostly whispers.

'Hello?' said a voice from the landing. 'Is there anybody there?'

He was shaking now.

He could see light coming through the cracks around the door, and he could hear a key turning in the lock. Instinctively he tried to stand, but the corner was too cramped. So he crouched down again, curling himself up into an even tighter ball.

Suddenly the door opened with a rush of light. He gripped his walking-stick and watched as a dark figure entered. It was carefully wheeling something into the room.

The figure made its way towards the window, where it paused for a moment in the shadows. He could see who it was, despite the gloom.

But all that did was make it worse.

2

I HEAR YOU KNOCKING

'Good morning, George. How are you feeling today?'

The loud but lacklustre female voice bellowing through the Tannoy caught him every time. He yawned, stretched and rubbed his eyes, then pressed the small red button beside his bed. 'I'm feeling on top of the world,' he replied, speaking into the tiny microphone just above the red button. 'Everything is fine and dandy.'

'And did you sleep well?'

'Er, yes. Very well indeed. As usual.'

'That's good then,' said the voice, slightly dismissively. 'Now *you* have a great day, won't you?'

There was a clicking sound. George breathed a sigh of relief. The voice had gone, along with its redundant sentiment. He would now be able to hear it through the thin plasterboard walls, asking his neighbouring inmates the very same questions. After that, the voice would slowly fade as it worked its way through all the poky ensuite rooms.

He remembered hearing it for the first time, how he'd jumped, assuming it was from the Other Side, a restless spirit come to cajole him as restless spirits often did. It wasn't a ghost, though. It was more frightening than that – it was chubby Pearl from reception. Equally elusive, rarely seen – and even then only in the early morning when the front desk was intermittently staffed.

He'd lied to her, of course. He'd had a terrible night, blighted by ghastly dreams and visions. But you had to be careful when addressing the Tannoy. If there was the slightest sign of discomfort then someone would come knocking at the door within minutes, sticking their patronizing nose in. So he answered the disembodied voice in exactly the same way every morning. It was like that at Bayview. They cared, dammit. It was their motto. It was emblazoned on the sign next to the entrance, above the bleak manicured bushes: 'Bayview Retirement Home – Putting Care First'.

He yawned again and stretched his limbs, alerting his body to imminent movement. He could see the daylight eating away at the edges of the dust-laden curtains. There was no hope of getting back to sleep now, however tired he might be. The birds were already screeching in the scrawny trees, which had been transplanted fully formed from a garden centre in the 1990s when Bayview had been built, making it look like a flimsy low-budget set for a situation comedy. There was no bay and no view. It was a dispiriting, purpose-built care home for the elderly, an oasis for the infirm. A plushed-up prefab in a God-forsaken cul-de-sac. He'd been trying to get used to the place ever since he'd been dragged here that fateful day, but it was no use. He'd even tried singing 'Home Sweet Home' every morning, over and over – often to the dismay of others – but it hadn't worked. It was about as effective as a slave singing 'My Way'. Besides, he was convinced that the word 'home' in the context of Bayview was an acronym for House of Mephistopheles' Employees. The Devil was residing somewhere in the building, he was sure of it.

He crawled out of bed and slowly opened the curtains. They made the usual scraping sound as they revealed the usual scene, the characterless trees trying to give the austere forecourt some character, along with the dogs that patrolled the entrance, sniffing at the Tarmac. They'd appeared when George had first arrived at Bayview, as if they were keeping guard, or so his nurse Serena had told him.

Beyond the forecourt there were several dreary houses with grey windows and run-of-the-mill cars on cramped gravel drives and a tantalizing glimpse of normality in the shape of a pub on the corner, the Bartholomew Arms. If he strained he could even see Edmunds Cut Price Store (apostrophe-free) on the sparse high street where the local shops scraped by between the corporate bullies. It was a drab outlook, but he was luckier than some of the other residents whose windows gave them a full view of what was laughingly called the garden. A series of fifty-two little plots for anyone who wished to raise a shop-bought plant, all laid out with as much flair as a pie chart.

Still, he had to look on the bright side. The sky was blue, except for a few cirrus clouds that were slowly being blown into invisibility. It felt as if summer was in the air, with the buds already dreaming of becoming flowers. Yesterday it had been wet, and the sky had been grey and puffy like the duvet on his bed. Today, though, it was clear and sunny. Even the rain's calcium deposits on the double-glazed windows looked like fine lace – the kind of lace that Judy would have worn. If he stared hard enough he could even see what looked like a small handprint at the bottom of the window, as if a child had put its palm against the glass.

Now that he'd surveyed the landscape in detail he would begin busying himself, working his way around the room, refamiliarizing himself with his surroundings as he did every morning. Easing his psyche back into reality. Or, at least, that was the intention.

His mind was already beginning to stray into difficult places. It was the same every day – the battle to forget. The problem was that there was very little in this damned shoebox of a room to divert his thoughts. 'Tastefully decorated and furnished to a high standard' was how the promotional leaflets described the accommodation. Anaemic, insipid and offensively inoffensive was how George described it. He'd even tried livening the place up with some of his old drawings. Over the years drawing had helped him cope with the iniquities of life. Sadly, though, any pictures or words that he was now seen to produce were seized upon as therapeutic, so he'd shut up shop and hidden everything under the bed. Enforced 'reminiscence therapy', as Serena called it, was the last thing he needed. What he needed was to forget about the past, which was why he had reluctantly decided to 'blend in'.

Since his arrival a few weeks earlier George had rarely been out of his room, despite constant encouragement from Serena to visit the Palm Lounge on the ground floor. There, as the promotional literature put it, he would be able to 'meet up and chat with other residents' or perhaps take part in one of the 'many fun and informative daily activities', such as the history quiz or the First Byte computer class run by Ms Belinda Bond – Nobody Does IT Better. The thought of it made him feel nauseous.

Today, though, as vile as it sounded, he would be making his first trip downstairs to visit the lounge. It would be hell, of course, but he was starting to draw attention to himself by staying holed up in his room, and that wasn't part of the plan.

It might also stop people knocking on his door day and night, night and day. He could already hear movement outside in the corridor. It felt like the walls were closing in.

Perry, his neighbour to the left, had been knocking on a daily basis, bringing him various publications to read. Luckily he always had advance warning, with Perry coughing and clearing his throat in the corridor long before he knocked. This was a chance for George to prepare for the onslaught of third-rate impressions and random television catchphrases. 'Here's one I made earlier,' Perry would say, handing him a magazine, cracking his knuckles and briefly standing on tiptoe. 'It's quite a wrench to give you this, old man. But I know what it's like when you can't get around . . . Lovely jubbly.'

George always hoisted a smile and thanked Perry kindly, unsure which magazine he disliked the most – *Model Engineer*, *British Railway Modelling Monthly* or *Railway Modeller*. 'The thinking-man's alternative' to Serena's sensationalist weeklies and promotional pamphlets is what Perry called them. 'Never mind the propaganda,' he'd say with a wink as he stroked his moustache. 'Have a proper gander at these.' He made the same joke every time, laughing like a hyena then coughing like a consumptive. At which point George always covered his face. It was a small room after all.

George stood and looked at himself in the mirror. It was a task that had become more and more challenging over the years; partly through the physical encumbrance of his back, which forced him to look askance, but mainly down to the fact that he was slowly becoming a grey-haired fossil with a grandiose nose.

He was becoming vague, too – which was a polite way of putting it. His memory was not so much a sieve as a decrepit antique colander. This morning, for instance, he'd spent a disproportionate amount of time looking for his trousers before realizing that they were hanging on the back of his chair. The same farce was about to commence with his shirt, which he would eventually also find hanging on the back of the chair.

Serena was to thank for his clothing. When he had first arrived at Bayview she announced that she would take it upon herself to cheer him up. True to her word, the very next day she presented him with a bin-bag containing three pairs of what she called slacks, six-and-a-half pairs of socks, five shirts (one of which looked suspiciously like a blouse) and a selection of what seemed to be luminous underwear. He'd thanked her as best he could, quietly resigning himself to permanently wearing his pyjamas. However, fearing that this might be a conspiracy to keep him imprisoned at Bayview for ever, he had now decided to play them at their own game. He would see to it that the communal lounge would regularly be treated to the most offensive combination of clothing he could muster. Today it was pale-blue flares rolled up at the ankles, a bright-green tartan shirt and a pair of red-striped Nike trainers with padded rubber soles – the last of which had been donated by Perry.

There was a knock at the door. He felt his stomach tighten.

'Are you awake in there, young man?' It was Serena. She was the only person at Bayview for whom George did not nurture an instinctive hatred.

'Oh yes, I'm most definitely awake,' he said loudly. 'Doing my morning exercises . . . You can't come in, though. I'm not decent.'

'But, George, when are you ever decent?' There was laughter on the other side of the door, followed by a pause. 'Have you remembered to take your medication this morning?'

'Er, yes,' said George.

'You don't sound too sure. You know your pills are important.'

George had been given packet after packet of foil-wrapped tablets since his arrival at Bayview. He had even taken some of them, although the vast majority had been given to the increasingly soporific birds.

'All right, then. I'll take your word for it,' said Serena through the door. 'I'll be bringing your breakfast up soon, so don't do too much exercise – or *you'll* be bringing it up as well . . . Oh, and don't forget what day it is.'

'Is that a general comment?' enquired George. 'Or are you referring to something specific?'

'It was on the events list I gave you. It's Upton Tuesday.'

'Oh yes, and I'm very much looking forward to it. I'm all shook up, as you might say.'

'OK. Well, I'll go and get your breakfast then.'

George gave a thank-you grunt and sat down on the side of the bed. For the past two Tuesdays he'd heard the dull thump of amateur musicians and the low moan of geriatric Elvis impersonator Upton Silver resounding from the Palm Lounge downstairs. At first he'd tried covering his ears, thinking that it was the radio from one of his neighbours, but it hadn't worked. It was simply too loud – and his room was on the second floor.

He wasn't a big fan of the real Elvis Presley, and the idea of an OAP Elvis impersonator who was apparently in the habit of randomly serenading the residents appalled him. Serena had recounted an evening when the ersatz Elvis had sung 'Love Me Tender' in her ear from beginning to end. It was hardly an incentive for George to attend, but at least the occasion would take the spotlight off his Palm Lounge début. Which could only be good.

He looked at himself in the mirror, done up to the nines. He'd been lucky with his hair. He still had most of it, although it was grey and unruly; all he could do was train it to one side and hope for the best. Still, at least his hair had a life of its own, which was more than he had in this drab vanilla hellhole. That would end soon, though. His days at Bayview Retirement Home were numbered, and he would make sure of it. When the moment was right he'd make his way back home to his beloved Thade Street, where Judy would be waiting. Besides which, the Devil was resident somewhere in the building, and he didn't fancy sharing his lodgings with Satan.

There was a sudden flash in the mirror, as if something had run across the room. It looked like the figure of a small boy. George looked around. 'Tom?' he called out. 'Is that you?'

After a few moments a little boy in grey shorts and a blue jumper emerged tentatively from behind the chair.

'How long have you been there?' asked George. 'You gave me quite a shock.'

'Sorry. I didn't mean to scare you, pops.'

'Scare me? I said you gave me a shock. That's not the same thing at all.'

'Well, you looked like you were scared,' laughed the boy.

'It would take more than a little squib like you to scare me, young man.'

The boy smiled. His face was young and unmarked, although his brow was lined and his green eyes looked tired beyond his years. 'Well, I'm soooo sorry, pops,' he mocked.

George huffed and puffed theatrically for a few moments,

then smiled. 'Don't be sorry, matey. Keep creeping up on me like that and one day I might just be a goner.'

The boy looked shocked. 'Oh, you don't wanna be joinin' the likes of me again, do you?'

'No, not any more, Tom,' sighed George. 'I think I'm over that now.'

Tom had been a constant presence throughout George's life, both dead and alive, but he had only started making regular appearances here at Bayview, and George saw the visits as a blessing, the one drawback being that he always wanted to hug the little fellow. But that was something that he'd never be able to do again. It was one of the biggest regrets of his life.

'Shall we do a little jig, then?' asked Tom, adopting an athletic pose as if at a starting line.

'I'd love to, but I don't think I'm up to it.'

'Well, watch me, then,' said Tom as he started to hop around in a circle.

George tried mimicking him, but his rheumatism was rife, and what was once a sprightly step was now an apoplectic shuffle.

Suddenly there was another knock at the door. George stopped in his tracks.

'Hey, are you all right in there?' said a voice from the corridor. It was Serena again.

'Er, yes,' replied George, somewhat breathlessly.

'Well, you don't sound too good. I'm coming in. I've got your breakfast out here.' She unlocked the door and entered the room, wheeling a tired-looking food trolley. The air was immediately filled with the pungent smell of fried pig as George stood by the bedpost, still catching his breath. Tom, meanwhile, had hidden behind the chair – he was never sure who could see him. Peeping out, he gestured at Serena and crossed his eyes. She didn't flinch. Clearly he was invisible to her.

'Such a lot of noise,' said Serena. 'You know you shouldn't be overdoing it, not in your condition.' She began uncovering the plates. 'Look, I've brought you a bacon sandwich. I know you like them.'

George sat down in the chair beside the window and carefully took the tray from her.

'I'll leave the tea here on the trolley,' she said, fearing third-degree burns. Serena, with her specially designed cut-price blouse and slacks, always looked as if she was wearing pyjamas. They were the fashion equivalent of the Bayview building and the obligatory apparel of the home's nurses.

'I'm sorry about the noise earlier,' said George. 'I was just a little overexcited, it being Upton Tuesday and all.'

'Well, it is quite an event,' said Serena, glancing at his shirt and trousers. 'So, is this your outfit for Upton then?'

'You guessed it. Thought I'd make an effort. It's now or never.'

'And did I give you these?' she asked, picking up the striped Nike trainers.

'No, they were Perry's. What do you think?'

There was a pause. 'Well, you've got all the colours of the rainbow here, haven't you? You'll certainly stand out.'

'Thanks.' To stand out was his intention; today was the day when it would all start. 'This is a lovely breakfast, by the way,' he said obsequiously. 'A grand start to the day. So what's on the menu for this afternoon?'

Serena smiled. 'Well, we'll have to wait and see,' she said, pausing at the door on her way out. 'You know, George, we really are all looking forward to seeing you downstairs today. You will come down, won't you?'

George nodded. He definitely would.

He looked at her full red lips as she stood there at the door as if posing for a painting. They were lush against her soft brown skin, and for a moment he wished she was fifty years older.

She smiled at him briefly. 'I'll be back,' she said in a thick German accent as she closed the door.

And the spell was broken.

3

SEND IN THE CLOWNS

The moment had come. George was now downstairs in the hall, having parked himself beside the lifts. From where he was standing he could see the reception area through the window walls and the automatic glass door. It was deserted as usual, like a border control without any visible guards, although it was allegedly spied on by CCTV.

He looked at the sign beside the communal notice board. Large black letters for the visually impaired loomed above a severed hand, which was pointing to a room full of chairs: 'This Way to the Palm Lounge'. The font was plain and characterless – no flourishes, no style. It seemed more like an omen than a direction to an airless room full of old people. But then anything gained meaning if George looked at it for long enough. It was part of being old. The more experience and knowledge you brought to something, the more it seemed to be connected with everything else, and that was fatal. It silted up the brain and left you rooted to the spot, snarled up in a grid of never-ending thoughts. It was happening now as he looked for hidden meanings in this perfectly ordinary sign. It had twenty-two letters. That was his room number. It was also the tarot number for the Fool – that was mere coincidence, of course.

Lunch had been and gone and was now lingering in the corridors, which were thick with the stench of shepherd's pie and warm upholstery, like a belch with a hint of bleach. He gripped the handrail, which ran the length of the corridor, to steady himself. It was more than mere physical support – it was emotional succour. He'd skilfully managed to delay this dreaded moment until the early afternoon, but the time had finally arrived, and he was just minutes away from bantering with old bastards and fending off the nudge-nudge nattering of ancient biddies. Not to mention the blaring television. He could already hear them all plonked in front of the soma screen, laughing at nothing. Making noises to show everyone, including themselves, that they were still alive. Those that weren't laughing would probably be staring hopelessly into middle distance, wondering where the hell they were and when they were going to leave.

As he stood there in the hall all he could think of was that dreadful night when they had dragged him from the Thames. It was only a short walk to the river from his house in Thade Street, and it was a journey he'd made thousands of times. This time, though, he'd been reluctant to leave the house, knowing that he would be closing his front door for the last time.

He remembered looking around the rooms, briefly switching on the lights and saying his goodbyes. He could feel all the memories in the walls. He could hear noises in the nooks and crannies, in league with the half-light and the shadows. It was as if, somehow, all the years had gathered and were now waiting to bid him farewell. All the people from all the moments stopped in their tracks and waved him off. Saluting him, wishing him good luck, *bon voyage*, *au revoir*,

God go with you, been nice knowing you, *bon appétit* . . . All his memories were there, and he was saying goodbye to each and every one of them.

He'd originally planned to throw himself from the bridge, taking in the air before heading down into watery bliss, but when he saw that the tide was out he'd decided to make his way down to the stony beach instead. He'd approached the algae-ridden river steps with caution, fearing that the slippery leather soles of his fur-lined boots might let him down. Nothing could be more humiliating than failing at suicide, surely. Having reached the beach, he'd stumbled over the debris to the water's edge and had sunk slowly to his knees. It was dark, and he could feel the ice-cold water seeping through his silken trousers. The sirens and the shouts from passers-by were all around him now as he rolled into the river and the icy water began to envelope him . . .

'Nice to see you, to see you nice,' said a voice, suddenly beside him in the hall.

George jumped. It was Perry. His pallid face was the same colour as the wallpaper. Both had subtle patterns on a pasty background, presumably washable in case of accidents.

'Great to see you on the ground at last,' said Perry, straightening his tie, which hung down over his beach-ball belly. 'And I must say I do like your outfit. Particularly those red running shoes.' He stood on tiptoes for a moment and cracked his knuckles, not for the first time.

'Well, I'm glad you approve. I do think they go rather well with the tartan shirt and pale-blue trousers.'

'You'll put Upton to shame, and he always wears a rhinestone suit,' said Perry, checking his watch. 'He's not on for another two hours, forty-seven minutes and thirty-eight seconds, but would you like me to escort you to the Palm Lounge, sir?'

George shook his head emphatically and looked awkwardly at the notice board.

'You talkin' to me?' said Perry. 'Ooh, you are awful, but I like you.'

George's instinctive desire to be excluded was growing by the second. He could now hear the clanking of cups and saucers from the lounge and a pompous man talking loudly about nothing. He had to ignore it, though. The Palm Lounge was all part of the plan.

'Tell you what,' said George. 'Why don't you go ahead and find us both a seat?'

'No worries, mate,' said Perry in an atrocious Australian accent. 'I suppose there's a while to go, and no one ever really turns up for the matinée . . .' There was an embarrassing pause as he stared at George.

'Honestly,' said George. 'You go on ahead. Please. I'll make my entrance in a couple of minutes.' He began avidly reading the advertisements on the board, along with the requests from residents and staff, hoping to bore Perry into leaving him alone. He was feeling nervous now, like a dog at the mouth of a cave. It was his only way out, though, to blend and then scarper. It was all part of the master plan. If you wanted to beat them you had to join them first.

Jan at Number 17 has a portable transistor radio for sale. Note: please contact her at the weekend, as she would like to hear the end of this week's *Book at Bedtime*. After that she's going digital. £5 ono

He could feel Perry's breath on the back of his neck. What do I have to do to make him go away? he wondered.

We kindly request that if you are disposing of unwanted copies of Yellow Pages directory books, please place them in the Unwanted Yellow Pages Directory Books Box and we will get rid of them properly. We don't want another December on our hands. Thanx.

He tried summoning a fart. It would take a few moments.

SPECIAL ANNOUNCEMENT: We are very pleased to welcome back acclaimed Elvis impersonator Upton Silver! He will be doing two shows next Tuesday – a matinée at 3.30 p.m. and a late show for all you night owls at 8.00 p.m. If you really want to get All Shook Up, please feel free to attend both! There is no admission charge.

Serena was now standing behind him, too. The game was up.
'Well, look who it isn't,' said Serena. 'Come on in, yer daft ha'porth. Stop reading this fascinating notice board and let me introduce you to everyone. You, too, Perry.' George smiled weakly as she grasped him firmly by the shoulders and guided him towards the lounge, pausing theatrically in the doorway while Perry secured a seat at the reading-table.

George looked around the room. Every expense had been spared, and the cut-price newness was being exposed by the rare but unforgiving glare of the sunlight. The thin carpet was a dirty brown, punctuated by palms, undernourished but pulling through. The flimsy walls, which you could kick down with a bit of rage and some fair-sized hobnail boots, were a dirty beige. The ceiling looked as if it had been varnished with golden syrup, while cheap brass chandeliers dangled tantalizingly above the chairs, which had been hastily rearranged to make way for the temporary stage which was tastelessly decorated and seemingly composed of duckboards and upended boxes. The velveteen curtains were a bleached puce, laden with frills and dusty pelmets, while the grey nylon nets embroidered with vague flowery shapes thankfully obscured the view of the garden. But then, perhaps this was all part of the plan. After all, beauty is the last thing you want to see when you're on your way out. It only makes leaving all the more painful.

'Look, everyone,' proclaimed Serena, beaming as if she was at a children's party. 'This is Mr George Pemberton. He's been with us for a while, but this is his first visit to the Palm Lounge. So please make him feel at home.'

The inmates all gazed at him with the same defeated look that zoo animals give you from their cages. Perhaps it was the pale-blue slacks and tartan shirts. George looked at them all done up like a dog's dinner as if they were going somewhere special, only to trundle downstairs to peer slack-jawed at ancient sitcoms and property programmes. It seemed like some kind of cruel experiment. All of them staring defeat in the face; a sea of white hair and glasses. Creatures kept alive long after their natural lifespan by force-fed diets and endless medication; made to witness their own physical decline while staggering under the burden of ever-increasing memories.

'Well, he's obviously dressed up for the occasion, hasn't he?' said an old woman with short white hair and big eyes. 'Nice flares. Bit short for you, aren't they? You look like a clown. I like your shoes, too. I know all about shoes. I used to live in a basement flat.'

George looked at the woman in her bright-red cardigan, over-sized and sagging, and her pink leather shoes, which would have been more suited to a schoolgirl. But he made no comment.

'By the way,' she continued, 'if the TV's too loud it's tough, because this is one of my favourite programmes. And don't tell me I can watch it on the watch-again thing because we don't get that here.'

'Er, let me introduce you to the lovely Clarissa,' said Serena. 'And we *can* get catch-up TV, it's just that Clarissa's forgotten how to work it.'

Clarissa frowned and looked at George. 'You're the one who was rescued, aren't you? Honestly, I can't imagine going through what you went through. I have to talk myself out of a panic when I put my jumper on inside out. You know, you do look like that fellow on the television. In the face, I mean . . . You know the one . . .'

There was a long pause. Perry coughed, briefly hoisting himself up on to his toes.

'OK, Clarissa,' said Serena. 'Do let us know when you've worked out who you're talking about. In the meantime, George, that's June over there.' She gestured towards a solid-looking woman in a headscarf sitting in the corner of the room. 'She likes her headscarves, does June.'

'Keeps my wig on,' said June.

Perry coughed again. 'June loves to talk. Don't you, June?'

'I do,' she said emphatically, staring at George with rock-hard eyes. Even from where he was standing George could see that she was vividly made-up, with scarlet lips and jet-black eyebrows painted on a powder-pale face.

'Oooh, George,' said Perry, holding up a copy of *OK!* magazine. 'Madame said "I do". I think that means that you two are now married. Perhaps you'll be on the cover of this lovely magazine next week.'

George nodded. He was starting to feel claustrophobic not to mention angry. To calm himself he imagined Judy's brides-dogs Burt and Hal growling at Perry and snapping at his ankles, and the anger was replaced by joy.

'Good old Perry, he's always ready for a joke,' said Serena with an insincere laugh. 'And now may I introduce you to the lovely Bernard.'

'Charmed, I'm sure,' said a tall willowy man in a blazer who was drinking a cup of tea. He lifted the cup and winked, before putting it back on the saucer, placing it on the table and rising to his feet. This was the pompous man George had heard earlier talking about nothing. 'I'm old, I'm old. I'll wear my trouser bottoms rolled,' he continued as he offered George his hand. George looked at him quizzically while his hand remained firmly by his side. 'It's T.S. Eliot,' said Bernard, winking again. 'I was referring to your rather memorable clothing.'

George already felt like punching Bernard, and he'd only just met him.

'Well, what's wrong with rolled-up flares?' asked Clarissa, frowning. 'And anyway he looks like that fella. You know, that funny-looking hunchback . . . Takes his clothes off when the writing comes up.'

'Er, I can only apologize,' said Bernard, sitting down again and reaching for his cup and saucer. 'Clarrie. Nobody knows what you're talking about . . . Just for a change.' The last four words were muttered from behind the cup.

'Who you calling Clarrie?' said Clarissa. 'And why did she say "Mr" anyway when she introduced him? I didn't think he was a "Mrs". Although I suppose he could be one of those queer fellas. Like that one who heard it through the grapevine, hiding in the bushes.'

'Do you mean Marvin Gaye?' said Serena. 'He was heterosexual. That was just his name.'

'Like Roger Moore,' said Perry, clearing his throat. 'That's not a name. That's an ambition.'

In a desperate measure George now began shifting quietly across the lounge, seemingly unnoticed, faking interest in the makeshift duckboard stage. He stood and stared at two tired-looking Hawaiian garlands draped on either side of a banner that read 'Welcome to Upton Silver'. He was trying to imagine the legendary Upton shuffling on, wearing an old rhinestone suit. Anything was more pleasurable than listening to his fellow inmates indulging in their 'fun and informative daily activities'. So far, his visit to the Palm Lounge hadn't helped his state of mind. He was beginning to loathe the place, with its stinking corridors and compost-coloured carpets, even more than before.

'So who wants a cup of tea, then?' asked Serena, feigning enthusiasm.

'Don't mind if I do,' said Perry, slyly taking the television remote and reducing the volume. 'Builder's cuppa and a dash of milk, please. Silver top if possible.'

'It was that Perrin fella,' said Clarissa. 'That's who it was. Took his pants off on the beach. That's who he looks like. And he was also in that advertisement for drinking, along with that slapper. Oh God, you know the one.'

'So who else would like a cup of tea, then?' asked Serena, inches from the end of her tether.

'She had a sister,' sniffed Clarissa. 'Another slapper . . .'

'Very good,' said Bernard. 'Now, would you like a cup of tea, Clarissa my dear? The lovely Serena is asking.'

'Are you trying to chat me up?' frowned Clarissa. 'Do you want to have it off?'

'Nothing was further from my mind. I was merely seeing if you wanted a cup of cha.'

'Well, that's nice, isn't it? I mean, I might need lubing up downstairs, but it all works. I'm sure the slapper twins need a bit of lube nowadays, too.'

'And what about you, George?' said Bernard, taking the helm. 'Cup of tea, old boy?'

George shook his head.

'Look, why don't I just bring a tray in?' sighed Serena, making her way out to the kitchen. 'And then perhaps Bernard can start reading us some of his poems.'

'Poems?' said George, wandering back towards the chairs.

'Yes. She said poems,' said Clarissa, suddenly getting up and making her way towards the door as fast as she could.

'Er, where are you going, Clarrie?' asked Bernard.

'I've forgotten the pickled onions . . .' said Clarissa, pausing briefly at the door. 'Bloody little bastards.'

Drawing found in Room 22,
Bayview Retirement Home

Untitled (written on the back: 'Are you sitting comfortably?'), undated

4

STUCK IN THE MIDDLE WITH YOU

George was standing by the window, looking out at the pie-chart garden. He was already planning an early exit from the Palm Lounge. The thought of Bernard reciting his poems was more than he could stomach. But, then again, the idea of sitting up in his room all afternoon brooding over the various thumps and bumps, not to mention his neighbour's blaring radio, was hardly inspiring either.

Clarissa had finally returned from upstairs and was now sitting in one of the chairs in her sagging scarlet cardigan, nursing a jar of pickled onions.

'Why don't you come over here and sit down?' she said, waving at George.

George tore himself away from the window and wandered over to the cheap chairs. He could see Bernard at the reading-table. He'd ousted Perry from his perch and was making himself comfortable, preparing to recite his poems.

'So why've you got a jar of pickled onions?' he said, as he sat down.

'Oh, they're for Bernard's poems,' replied Clarissa. 'I thought I'd contribute something, rather than just sit there like Her Majesty.' She pointed towards June, who was slowly solidifying in her headscarf. 'I found them in my cupboard. I think they're about to go off.' She squinted at the label. 'I've always thought that they were going to outlive me. Don't know why.'

George was baffled but intrigued. Perhaps the Palm Lounge was the best bet after all.

After a few minutes Bernard cleared his throat and shuffled his papers like a headmaster sitting at his desk. George studied him for a moment. He had looked familiar from the moment he first saw him. He had one of those faces. Serious by default, with jowls that would judder as he walked. He cleared his throat again.

'Er, hello, everyone,' he said at last, rather stiffly. 'We're gathered here today so that I can read you some of my new poems, which I'm proudly submitting to the much-acclaimed *Help the Aged Golden Poetry Collection.* I'd love to know what you, my public, think of them. The truth is, *j'écris un peu* . . . I dabble. Although perhaps it's more like rhyming Scrabble.' He paused for a moment.

'Was that one of the poems then?' said Clarissa. 'If so it was rubbish. Mind you, I'm not good with words. For years I thought *Roget's Thesaurus* was a Froggy children's story about a boy and a dinosaur.'

'No,' said Bernard, 'that wasn't a poem. It was just a little live rhyme, you might say.' He winked and gave a smug smile.

'Or you might not,' said Perry, rustling his newspaper from a chair near by.

'Well, go on then,' said Clarissa. 'Just read the bloody thing before we all fall asleep. How about that one you gave me the other day?'

'Oops. Too much information,' said Perry, burying his head in his paper.

'Do you mean "Feeling Up"?' said Bernard. Perry grimaced. 'Very well then,' he said, clearing his throat. 'I wrote this for a certain someone. It's not very long.'

'That's not what I've heard,' said Clarissa.

Bernard ignored her and began.

> 'When I wake up with a hangdog face
> And look around this plaintive place
> I think of you beside me
> And know that in my heart reside thee
> That is when I start
> Feeling up, feeling up, feeling up
>
> 'With my spirit rising
> The moment needs baptizing
> So I wander to the tea and kettle
> Feeling in fine fettle
> Where I make a cup
> To celebrate the fact that I am
> Feeling up, feeling up, feeling up
>
> 'You to me are all I need
> The book that I can sit and read
> The wound that thence starts healing
> That makes my heart start
> Feeling up, feeling up . . . feeling up.'

As usual, whenever Bernard finished reading one of his poems there was a terrible silence.

'Well,' said Clarissa. 'Doesn't that bring tears to your eyes?'

'It certainly does,' said George, trying not to laugh as he

pretended to wipe something from his trousers. He was starting to dislike Bernard on an epic scale.

'Thank you very much, George,' said Bernard. 'That's much appreciated. You're obviously a man who likes the finer things in life. I think you'd agree there was definitely more than a touch of Larkin in there.'

'And a big lump of Ayres,' said Perry, still rustling his paper.

George could now feel a large fart brewing in his bowels. It was perfect timing.

'Oh, do that one called "It's Getting Harder",' said Clarissa, fondling the jar in her lap. 'It's just so sad.'

Bernard cleared his throat. 'I shall satisfy requests anon. In the meantime this is called "Love Song". It's new, and I hope you get the reference . . .

> 'Let us go then, you and I,
> Go and buy some shepherd's pie
> We have nothing but a list
> And the mist hath cleared to see us through
> Along the High Street
> O, the High Street

> 'Shepherds delight is what they say
> When the sky is high at end of day

> ''Tis when we eat our rations
> That we feel our vibrant passions
> Oh, as if behind us comes a ghost a-crawlin'
> Not afeared to talk of death with noble breath
> Goodbye, goodbye, tatty-bye, all
> O, tatty-bye.'

Again there was silence, followed by a dull thump beneath George's buttocks. It was accompanied by him grunting and tilting slightly in the chair. A look of mild relief briefly crossed his face.

'Did you just break wind, George?' asked Perry, taking cover behind a Sunday supplement.

George nodded. 'Don't worry. I'll sit on it.'

'I do hope you said "sit". When you get up that chair will stink like a corpse now.'

'But it already does.'

'That's probably because you've been sitting in it.' Perry looked at Bernard. 'There you go, Bernie Boy. Rhyme something with "corpse". There's a challenge for you.'

'They used to call him king of hearts,' said Clarissa, fondling her jar of pickled onions. 'Now they call him king of farts . . . Look at me. I'm a poet and I didn't know it.'

Bernard frowned. 'So, anyway, did anyone get the reference?'

'I thought it was that old TV programme *One Man and His Dog*,' said George. 'With the shepherds and everything.'

'Eliot, T.S.,' said Bernard, winking with a smug smirk.

'Dick, U.R.,' murmured George. He farted again. There was no grunt this time, just a smile and a sigh of satisfaction.

Bernard stood up. At first he tried to lean forward and put his liver-spotted hands on the table in a gesture of authority. But this proved too awkward, so he settled for folded arms and a frown. 'Don't take your ignorance out on me, Mr Pemberton,' he sneered.

'Why not?' said George. 'You just did by reading that.'

There was a sudden yell from the corner of the room. It was June. 'Just get out of here!' she shouted. 'I don't care how troubled you are.'

The room seemed to freeze for a moment as everyone stared at her.

'Are you all right there, old girl?' ventured Perry, putting down his paper.

'I'm not talking to you,' barked June, slowly raising her hand and pointing at the wall directly in front of her. 'It's him I'm talking to.'

'But . . . there's nobody there,' said Perry. 'It's a wall.'

George suddenly felt anxious. He remembered crouching in the darkness, huddled in the corner, trying not to be seen. Trembling at the sounds all around him, with the crude sketch of a room slowly becoming visible. Sideboard, bed, bookshelves, chairs, the usual roll-call . . .

Serena suddenly appeared from the kitchen carrying a tray full of cups. 'All right, everyone. Don't panic,' she said, placing the tray noisily down on the table. 'Thank you very much, Bernard, for your lovely poems. Now, how about some more tea and telly, folks?'

'What about my pickled onions?' demanded Clarissa. 'Can someone please check the sell-by date?'

'I'd be happy to,' said George, leaning across. Clarissa handed him the jar.

'Er, will that be one lump or two, George?' enquired Serena, clanking the cups and pouring the tea.

'Don't tempt me,' said George, as he peered at the label while secretly loosening the lid. Bernard was a major source of irritation, and he needed to be scratched. Flatulence was not enough – he needed knocking from his pedestal. As ever, George would need a weapon to see off intruders, and his slap-stick wasn't to hand. The pickled onions would do nicely.

Serena turned on the television. After a few moments

normal programming was resumed, with June returning to her usual state of terminal introversion and Clarissa frowning at the soma screen. *Top of the Pops* was on, blaring pop music from the 1970s.

'Where's the one that sings but sounds like he shouldn't?' asked Clarissa. 'I used to like him.'

'Well, there are plenty of those,' said Perry, picking up his paper.

'You know the one. He sounds like an old woman who should go to the doctor.'

'Do you mean Billie Holiday?' said Perry.

'No, he's been gone for years. This one's got a wart. Don't know why he couldn't get it seen to. I mean, he must have a bob or two.' She paused. 'Ah, yes, that's it . . . Bob Stewart.'

'You mean Rod,' said Serena, carefully distributing cups of tea.

'That's what I said,' frowned Clarissa. She pointed to the screen. 'And look at this lot. They're called the Floaters. That's like calling yourself the Shits. Nice song, though. Anyway, where are my bloody pickled onions?'

'I'm sorry,' said George. 'But my eyes aren't what they were. Better give them to Bernard.'

Clarissa sighed and hauled herself up out of her chair. 'Bloody onions,' she said as she passed the jar to Bernard.

'I think the date's on the bottom of the jar,' said George.

Bernard took the jar and turned it upside down. The entire contents flooded into his lap. 'Oh shit!' he said, standing up. His trousers were soaked through with vinegar as the onions rolled like rotten golf balls across the carpet. 'Excuse my fucking French!'

'I can't leave you lot alone for two minutes, can I?' said

Serena, rushing back into the room from the kitchen, her usual perfumed presence doused by the sickly sweet smell of vinegar. 'I've got clowns to the left of me, and, well, we've got Upton arriving in a couple of hours. Nobody touch anything. Let me get the cleaner in.'

'Well, someone's in a pickle,' said George, while Bernard worked his way through two dozen serviettes, hopelessly trying to wipe himself down. 'Poltergeist activity, I'll wager. One of June's friends, perhaps . . .'

Perry glanced briefly at George. He looked as if he was about to say something before burying his head in his paper again.

Clarissa was in a state. 'Oh, for God's sake, Bernard!' she said, getting up and flailing her arms as if the roof had fallen in. 'You'll never get the stink out of the bloody carpet. Let alone your trousers. And what about my onions?'

'I just don't know why I bother with you people,' snapped Bernard, storming out of the room. 'You can all go to hell.'

'Well, at least you were wrong about the onions,' said George, trying to keep a straight face. 'You're still alive, aren't you?'

'Only just,' said Clarissa.

George was beginning to feel much better than he had before. If fact, he almost felt like doing a little St Vitus's dance, if such a thing had been physically possible.

'This room is definitely jinxed,' said Clarissa, pacing around and tightening her baggy cardigan around her as if there was a chill in the air. 'I had a party in here once. It was a bloody disaster. Everyone had stickers with their names on, because nobody knew who anyone was. Problem was, no one could read them. So they all had to go upstairs to get their glasses. Most of them didn't come down again.' She sat back down, sinking into her chair with an air of defeat and staring into the middle distance. 'Can someone turn up the volume on the television, please?' she said at last. 'It's all I've bloody got.'

Perry did the honours, then moved across to talk to George.

'Actually, old boy,' said Perry, crouching down beside George's chair and offering him his newspaper, 'would you mind if I had a quick word?' He gestured towards the makeshift stage. George was intrigued. He took the paper, then got up and followed Perry to the other side of the room.

'What are you two scheming about over there?' asked Serena, picking up the pickled onions. 'I hope you're not planning anything.'

'No. We're just inspecting the stage,' said Perry. 'Don't want any more accidents, do we?' He leant towards George. He seemed a little nervous. 'Er, it's strange you should mention poltergeist activity before.' He lowered his voice. 'I mean, do you get a lot of, well, noise in your room? You know, thumps and bumps?'

George nodded. 'Yes, I do.'

'Well, it's just that I think that there's something here . . . In this place. I mean, you saw June over there. The other night – a particularly dark one if I remember rightly – I had a spot of bother. *British Railway Modelling Monthly*, March 1971 edition . . . Thrown right across the room.'

'And did you pull the red cord?'

'Well, yes, but I think they thought I was going a bit . . . you know.' Perry made a face and cracked his knuckles. There was an awkward pause. 'So anyway, I wondered if you could give me a hand, if you know what I mean.'

'What sort of hand?'

Perry looked over at Serena and smiled. 'Erm. Eight-letter word beginning with E.' He lowered his voice for effect.

'Earmuffs? Emulsion?'

'Listen very carefully. I shall say zis only once,' said Perry, before putting his hand to his mouth in an exaggerated pose and whispering, 'Exorcism.'

George was shocked. 'And what on earth makes you think I could do something like that?'

'Well, you just seem like the right sort of chap. To be honest, it's starting to get me down. Dark clouds gathering and all that.' Perry leant a little closer. George coughed slightly, reeling from the stench of his molars. 'You know, we've got to club together in a place like this,' said Perry. 'And I would definitely owe you one . . .'

George forced a smile. 'I'll think about it.'

'I must say, that's very generous of you,' said Perry, returning to his normal volume as they walked back towards the chairs. 'And do let me know what conclusion you reach.'

'Will do,' said George, sitting down.

'F-A-B.'

George was disturbed by Perry's odd request. He picked up the paper he'd left on the chair arm and stared vacantly at the newsprint. He was beginning to realize how shaken he'd been by June's outburst, and he was now in no doubt . . . The Devil really was alive and well – and living in Bayview.

5

ALWAYS ON MY MIND

George had given up staring at the newspaper. He was now standing in front of the makeshift stage again, looking at Upton's welcome banner complete with Hawaiian garlands. A sudden bout of spring sunshine was warming the lounge, highlighting the grubbiness of the windows and charging up the static in the manmade fibres, not to mention the few individuals still present in the room.

'She's a right trollop, she is,' said Clarissa, pointing to the cleaner as she left the lounge with a bucketful of sickly smelling suds. 'Used to wear flip-flops all the time. Never mind the weather. Right slapper.'

'She's done a good job on the pickled onions, though,' said Perry, rifling through the magazines on the tea table. 'What do you think, George?'

'It's the little things, isn't it?' said George vaguely, as he stared at Upton's banner.

Clarissa now turned her attention to the television. 'I can't understand a bloody word they say nowadays,' she said, gesturing at the screen. 'I mean, what the hell are they going on about? And look at them, all dressed up in black with only their eyes showing. Are they Muslims or something?'

'No,' sighed Perry, flicking through a copy of *Mature Times*.

'They're penguins. It's a children's programme called *Pingu*.'

'Penguins?' Clarissa sighed and briefly looked down at her lap. 'That's such a shame. Like that hedgehog on the news.'

Perry looked baffled. 'What hedgehog?'

'You know. Got his head stuck in a tin of carrots. In a right fix he was.'

Perry shook his head. 'Why, oh why . . .' he said to himself.

'Shouldn't that be "how"?' asked George.

'I suppose so. Although it wasn't really a question. More a vague cry of desperation. Here's lookin' at you, kid.'

'I had a fish like that once,' continued Clarissa. 'Died when it was small. Found it floating on its side, poor thing. Called it Goldie. Never knew whether it was a woman or a man. Must have been lonely. Should have treated it better, though. Just never took the time . . . It was all my fault . . .'

'I had some fish once,' said June, suddenly stirred into action in the corner of the room. 'They ate each other.' There was a pause, as always whenever she decided to speak. 'Then my bloody folding walking-stick folded itself up while I was walking, didn't it?' There was another pause, even longer than before.

'Well, June, thank you for your words of wisdom,' said Serena, appearing from the kitchen with yet another tray. 'Answers on a postcard please . . . Empties anyone?' She offered up the tray. 'Just to let you know, Upton will be on stage in about forty minutes. We'll be bringing in a few more chairs, and we'll have to put a towel down there.' She pointed at the pickled-onion patch. 'Also, young Karel will be coming in very soon to start setting up – so don't be shocked if somebody under the age of seventy enters the room. OK, everyone?'

'I think it's Karel you need to warn,' said George, still staring at the stage.

Serena gave him a look of defeat before picking up some cups and heading back towards the kitchen.

'Oops, don't forget to set the youth alarm then,' said Clarissa. 'Somebody who doesn't remember the war is about to enter the building. Somebody moving more than a yard a minute. Red alert. Repeat . . .' She floundered. 'Repeat . . . er, whatever it was I just said.'

Perry stood up and brushed himself down. 'Well,' he said, briefly stroking his moustache, 'I think this is my cue to retire forthwith and don my smoking-jacket. You coming, George?'

'In a minute.' George made his way back to the chairs.

'Don't panic,' said Perry, before saluting and leaving the room.

'In the meantime, you can sit next to me,' invited Clarissa.

'Why not indeed?' said George, lowering himself into the chair beside her.

'I don't think we got off to a very good start, did we?' said Clarissa. 'Was I a bit rude?'

'Well, you were a bit off. But only at first.'

'I do like your trousers, though. They're the same colour as the sky. When it's nice, I mean. Like it is today.'

'Thank you,' said George. 'But don't let the sunshine fool you.' He pointed to the banner hanging across the stage. 'It says "Welcome to Upton Silver" . . . or, as I read it, "Evil Plot Now Comes True".'

Clarissa looked confused.

'It's an anagram.'

'What's an anagram?'

'It's when you rearrange the –'

'I know what an anagram is, you shit. I meant *where*'s the anagram.'

'On the banner,' said George, pointing at the stage.

'That sounds like Esperanto,' frowned Clarissa. She leant forward in her chair and looked him right in the face. 'Are you a bloody spy or something?'

George looked around the room theatrically. 'Well, if you promise not to tell . . .'

'Of course I won't, you prick.'

He leant forward and whispered in her ear. She smelt of hairspray.

'Well, I can't hear that, can I?' she grimaced. 'Who do you think I am, the Bionic Woman?'

He tried again, a little more loudly this time. 'I said no, I'm not a spy.'

'But you look like you're in disguise. Like that bloody puppet . . . You know, the clowny one with the slapstick. And you've got a bit of a stoop.'

George felt a sudden wave of anxiety wash over him. For some reason he was deeply disturbed by Clarissa's words.

Serena entered the room again, this time carrying two chairs. 'Come on, kids. Upton's now in the building, and Karel will be here in a couple of minutes. It's action stations.'

'Yes, well,' said George, getting up. 'I think I'd better go upstairs then and change my clothes. It's probably for the best, don't you think? I don't want to look like a puppet now, do I?'

Clarissa looked up at him. For the first time she seemed vulnerable.

'Don't worry. I'll see you in a little while,' said George with a smile.

He could see tears welling up in her eyes as she tried to smile back.

'I hope so,' she said. 'I really do.'

Clarissa was alone now. Serena had turned off the television, helped June to the door and filled the room with chairs. The Palm Lounge wasn't known for its vigour. It was a waiting-room devoid of atmosphere, offering up free copies of *Mature Times*. Few of the residents made it part of their daily routine, and who could blame them? Now, though, it seemed cold and even bleaker than usual, despite the spring sunshine and the makeshift stage complete with Hawaiian garlands. Clarissa looked at the banner draped across it. Perhaps George had been right about the subtext.

A young man suddenly entered the room carrying two big black cases. He was wearing a baseball cap back to front with a short blond ponytail sticking out beneath the brim. He rocked slightly as he walked, and his trousers looked as if they were too big for him. He smiled briefly at her. She returned the smile and found herself watching him as he carefully laid out the contents of the cases on the floor.

'Are you Karel?' she asked.

The young man looked up, slightly surprised. 'Er, yeah?' he said, a little shyly.

'Well, that's a lovely necklace you're wearing,' said Clarissa.

'Oh, dis.' He fingered the chain around his neck. 'Is not reeelly ah necklace.'

'Is it bing, then?' said Clarissa. 'I've heard about that on the radio. There used to be a singer in my day, he was called Bing, too. Didn't wear any jewellery, though. Wasn't really the fashion back then.'

'Ah fink you mean bling,' said Karel.

'Well, what did I say then?'

'Bing, Ah fink,' he said, making his way towards the door

before briefly stepping out into the hall. He returned a few moments later carrying two loudspeakers.

'Is this what you want to do, then?' asked Clarissa. 'Carry things around and then unpack them? A clever boy like you . . .'

'What d'ya mean?' replied Karel, unravelling a seemingly endless wire from one of the black cases.

'I mean, do you have any other ambitions?'

'Yeah. Ah wanna be a barista.'

'Really?' said Clarissa. She seemed shocked. 'Well . . . are you studying? It's very hard work being a barrister.'

'Nah. Is easy. Mah mate is one. He's tryin' to get me in der.'

'Well, I don't think it's as easy as you think, you know . . . People study to be barristers for years.'

'Nah, man. Is real easy. Is just servin' people and doin' yor bes' for dem.'

'Well, that's a very noble way of looking at it,' said Clarissa, lifting herself up out of her chair. 'But I don't think you'll be allowed to wear jewellery on the job.'

'Mah mate does . . .'

'Well, I suppose times do change,' she sighed, slowly making her way towards the door. 'I can't keep up. I'm just an out-of-date old crone . . . And I'm sorry if I made you feel second best, by the way.'

'Nah, is OK,' said Karel, still unravelling the wire. 'You is a niiice laydee wiv lots of experience.'

Clarissa paused in the doorway and looked at Karel for a moment. 'Well, thank you,' she said. 'That's very nice of you to say. I shall always remember that.'

The two of them smiled at each other. Karel had finally finished unravelling the wire. 'Is a pleasure, ma'am,' he said. 'Ah shall see you very soon.'

The Palm Lounge was filling up now, and George was looking out of the window again. At least the horticultural pie-chart offered some kind of relief from the slow-motion mayhem behind him. He had changed his clothes, opting for a dark-grey theme, although the red-striped Nike trainers with padded rubber soles remained. It was politics that had brought him back downstairs. All he needed to do now was lower his profile and blend into the background.

As he stood by the window he felt a hand on his shoulder. It was Perry, and he was pointing to what had now become a games table.

'Would you care to join me, old man, in a brief celebratory game of draughts?' he asked, looking at his watch. 'We've got seventeen minutes and fifty-eight seconds, by my reckoning.'

George nodded and sat down, unable to think of anything better to do.

'And don't mind me, will you?' said Clarissa, suddenly appearing beside them like a giant bird. 'I've brought my own sitting contraption.' She gestured to the footstool beside her.

'I thought you were finding a seat over there,' said Perry.

'Well, I found one here, didn't I, bell end?' said Clarissa, trying to make herself comfortable. The footstool was low, and the table was now level with her chest. It was a small table at best, made all the smaller when Clarissa leant forward and stared intently at the checked board in front of her.

'Well, as long as you don't make us lose our concentration,' said Perry. 'Blacks or whites, George? They're equal nowadays, so it shouldn't really matter. Don't want to show any prejudice.'

George rolled his eyes. 'Black, please.'

'You do know that he's *not* a spy, don't you?' said Clarissa, with an air of disappointment. 'At least he says he's not. But I suppose that's what spies say . . . He might be that puppet fellow, though.'

Perry smiled as he took the pieces out of the box. 'Well, that's a relief, eh, George? Not a spy. And who's this puppet chap?'

'I don't know what she's talking about,' said George, arranging the pieces on the board.

'Better not say anything,' said Clarissa, 'or he'll beat the shit out of you with his slapstick.'

'Well, that's the way to do it, eh, Mr Punch?' said Perry.

George tried to smile, but he was too irritated. He couldn't help feeling profoundly disturbed. And what was most disturbing was the fact that he didn't know why it was so disturbing.

The pieces were now laid out on the board.

'So, what are you actually playing, then?' asked Clarissa. 'It's not chess, is it? I mean, it's not Scrabble either. Why don't you play Monopoly instead?'

'It's draughts,' huffed Perry, making a move.

'That's not a game. That's a DIY problem. And anyway it's called checkers.'

'No. That's an Americanism. Either way, it takes a lot of concentration. Your move, George. I think you'll find mine's a good 'un.' He looked at his watch. 'Just under fifteen minutes before Mr Silver starts making his own moves, by the way.'

'Enough time to beat you, then,' said George, as he hopped over four of Perry's draughts.

'See. I told you,' said Clarissa.

'Cunning move,' said Perry. 'You really are a lot smarter than you look, eh, old man?'

The board suddenly darkened. It was Bernard blocking the light.

'Hope you don't mind my butting in,' he said, offering his

hand to George. 'Just thought I'd make peace with our new resident, Mr P. We all make mistakes, don't we? And it's only fair that I give you another chance.'

George reluctantly shook Bernard's hand.

'Splendid,' said Bernard. 'All's well that mends well . . . Now come, my dear Clarrie. I'm getting lonely. I believe it might be time for me to escort you to your seat. Upton and co are readying themselves for action.'

Clarissa sighed and got up from her footstool. 'He just wants my minge,' she said as she left. 'I can see his bulge from here.'

'It's the little things, isn't it?' said George.

'Ooh, George, you are awful, but I like you,' said Perry, saluting. He leant across the table, holding his hand to the side of his mouth in a gesture of secrecy. 'And I'm very glad to hear you're not a spy, by the way.'

The stench of Perry's molars once again engulfed George momentarily. 'I really don't know what she's talking about,' he said, feeling slightly sick. 'I think she's mad.'

'Don't panic. I'm only having a game with you, old boy.' Perry held up a draught. 'Or should I say, another game . . . ? My move, I think.'

George watched Perry's hairy hands as they hovered above the board. You could tell a lot from someone's hands. Like the bumps on their head or the way they moved. Perry kept his arms close by his sides when he walked and looked around him as he went. And then there was the missing ring finger. George had first noticed it when Perry had been plying him with magazines. 'It's why I never married,' Perry had joked, wiggling the stump one morning when he was delivering the latest issue of *British Railway Modelling Monthly*. 'Held a group of Nazis at gunpoint, don't you know. Book 'em, Danno, that's what I say.' All of which would have been fine had Perry actually been old enough to have been in the war.

'Your move,' said Perry, glancing at the makeshift stage beyond. Upton was imminent.

George pretended to study the board.

'Have you got any family, George?' asked Perry. 'Tell me a bit about yourself. I mean, are you married? I know that Punch fella had a wife called Judy . . . He used to hit her around something rotten, didn't he?'

George looked up at Perry with anger in his face. It was all he could do to stop himself from clamping his arms together and swinging them across the table like a club, knocking Perry off his perch.

'Steady on, old chap,' said Perry. 'Just joking.' He stiffened his neck and puckered his chin. 'A bit of controversy's a healthy thing, you know. I tell you, you've got to keep arguing in this place to stay alive.'

George looked back down at the board and took a deep breath. He closed his eyes and counted to ten. Judy would have been proud. 'Think about something you love, George,' she always used to say whenever anger threatened to engulf him. 'It will always make things better.' So he thought about her. But it only made things worse.

'Better make a move, old boy,' said Perry, leaning forward like a neurotic clerk. 'Time's running out, you know . . .'

'It certainly is,' said George, moving one of the black draughts at random. 'And, in answer to your question about my family, well, I'm not really sure I have any.' He feigned sadness. 'You see, I'm suffering from amnesia. At least, I think that's what they said.'

Clap! Clap! Clap!

Everyone looked around. Serena was standing in front of the makeshift stage, clapping her hands. Karel was behind her, tapping a humming microphone.

'Attention, everyone,' said Serena. 'Do please find your places before the chairs run out. Mr Upton Silver will be here in a few moments.'

Perry stood up from the table. 'Shall we call it a draw, old boy?'

George nodded. An old woman walked past them and glanced at the draughts. 'I'm off to the toilet,' she said. 'You can have my seat if you like. Won't be back for a while. These things take time.'

'Thank you kindly,' said Perry. 'Didn't she do well?'

Karel had now fixed the microphone and was standing in the middle of the makeshift stage. 'Hey, good day to all yoo haaaand dogs and teddy bears,' he boomed. 'Get ready to rock. Yor trip to Tennessee wiv Mister Upton Silver leaves in approximately tooo minutes.'

'But I put my name down for West Wittering,' said an anxious woman near the front. 'I don't want to go to Tennessee. That's in Scotland.'

'Shh!' hissed Serena, dishing out cushions. 'It's Upton time.'

Drawing found in Room 22,
Bayview Retirement Home

'Hound Dog', dated August 1971

6

DEVIL IN DISGUISE

The Palm Lounge was in semi-darkness. Upton was about to appear, and George was beginning to feel more than a little claustrophobic. Bernard had enticed Clarissa to the other side of the room, and George, for his sins, had ended up sitting next to June. A penumbral room full of old people is not the most inspiring place, but it's made even worse when you're stuck next to a black hole with scarlet lips and a powder-pale face. Indeed, it was a sign of the times that he felt reassured by Perry's presence in the neighbouring chair.

George couldn't help watching June out of the corner of his eye. She was rocking gently as if being blown by the wind. It made him feel queasy just to be near her. He sighed and closed his eyes. He could see ghostly faces at the windows, pressed up against the glass and struggling for air. He opened his eyes. The Palm Lounge suddenly seemed consoling, despite the fact that Serena was now going around the room and closing all the curtains, dragging them along the rails.

Soon a drum began to roll, followed by a tinny chunk of Elvis Presley's final single, 'Way Down'. The excerpt ended as abruptly as it began, just after the chorus.

Everyone stared at the empty stage.

Perry nudged George. 'It's now or never, eh?' he whispered.

There was an awkward pause before Upton finally appeared spotlit at the microphone in dark glasses and rhinestone suit. He slowly removed the glasses and studied the old folk in their seats.

'Stop your suspicious miiiiinds,' he drawled, pushing his chin into his neck to deepen his voice. It was a cross between Presley's sleepy Deep South accent and his own native Cornish brogue. 'Ya see, Ah can't help falling in love . . . My name's Upton Silver, good people. But lemme tell ya, Ah was born on the eighth day of January in the year of Our Lord 1947. And on the sixteenth day of August 1977, the very day the King passed away, Ah felt all shook up.' He shivered violently for emphasis. 'Ya see, Ah'd received a utility bill that very mornin',' he continued, 'and Ah looked at it. Yup, Ah looked at it haaaard, laydees 'n' gennulfolk. And Ah got wise. There it was in black 'n' white staring back at me. No, not "This bill is too much". Just my name: Mr U. Silver. Or, to put it another way, Mr U.R. Elvis. Yes, you are!'

He paused for dramatic effect and put his dark glasses back on, which was evidently the cue for a backing track to begin. George was suddenly interested. Anagrams had always fascinated him.

'And from that fateful day forward, good people,' continued Upton. 'Ah, yes, a fool such as Ah, have carried the King's message. So don't be cruel, let me be your good-luck chaaaaarm. And if you got a tale to tell, just ta-a-a-ake a walk down lo-o-o-o-onely street to heartbreak hotel.'

'What's he bloody talking about?' muttered June under her breath.

George ignored her, although Upton's spiel was making him feel a little tense.

'Get on with it,' someone shouted from the other side of the room.

Upton was crooning every song title now as he spoke, letting the sound waver out of him, shaking his head with the vibrato. 'Just let me take you back in tiiiiiiiime. Love meeee tenderrrr, love me sweeeet.' His zombie-like groans unfurled across the room. Then he lurched into three songs without a break – 'Don't Be Cruel', followed by 'One Night' and then 'Suspicious Minds' – striking poses throughout like an arthritic mime.

It was about halfway through the show that June began to get jittery. She'd been nodding to the songs with her eyes closed, tugging at her headscarf, and she'd even briefly joined in with the clapping during 'Don't Be Cruel' before it fell behind and faded as communal clapping always does. But she'd been talking incessantly to herself, repeating the same phrase over and over, 'You're not Elvis Presley, you're not Elvis Presley . . .'

The problem began when Upton was catching his breath between songs, addressing the honey-coloured ceiling. 'Are ya here with us now, Elvis? Are you lonesome tonight?'

'But it's the afternoon,' June had yelled suddenly.

Serena came as close to June as the chairs would allow and put her finger to her lips.

'I can feeeeeeeel the King,' crooned Upton, ignoring June's outburst as he paced up and down the small creaking stage, raising his arm to request some backing music. 'I can feel him, laydees 'n' gennulfolk. I can feeeeeel him. Elvis, show us the wonder of yoooou!'

'There's no bloody wonder in this place,' yelled June, desperately trying to stand. Her vividly made-up face, cruel and stony at the best of times, looked even more unnerving in the half-light.

'Surrender, good people,' proclaimed Upton, undeterred, rocking his head ecstatically as the backing music rapidly grew in volume. 'I'm a hunk, a hunk o' burning luuurrrrve . . . Yeah, a hunk, a hunk o' burning luuurrrrve.'

'No you're not,' snarled June. 'You're a lukewarm lump of shit!'

Serena stepped in and took June's arm, enticing her to stand before leading her slowly but steadily to the door. The old woman moved awkwardly, as if her body had been broken and put back together without reference to the manual.

'You walk like an angel,' sang Upton defiantly, unaccompanied at first until Karel, who was operating the equipment, found the right backing track. 'But I got wiiise . . . You're the Devil in disguuuuuuiiiise!'

Upton continued undaunted. George was relieved that June had left the lounge, but her presence lingered. He was haunted by her spiteful, vivid face. He knew that there was more to her than met the eye, and it had now been confirmed. After she'd left the room Upton sang her 'Devil In Disguise' theme tune again, pointing at George this time when he sang the line 'But I got wise'. It was as if he was addressing him personally.

Unable to bear any more, and inspired by Upton's coded message, George quit the darkened lounge soon after the first encore. He could hear the long goodbyes and sparse applause as he made his way back up to his room. He could also hear Serena coming up the stairs after him.

'Are you all right there, young man?' she asked, walking quickly up the corridor behind him.

'Yes, I'm fine,' said George, struggling to get his key into the lock. Privacy was what he needed now.

'Well, you don't want to overdo it, you know. Have you taken your medication? Let's face it, you're not one hundred per cent yet.'

'You're right, Serena,' sighed George, finally opening the door. 'I am utterly exhausted. I definitely need a rest, which is why I left so abruptly. I hope I wasn't rude.' He exaggerated his posture a little. 'In fact,' he continued, at the risk of laying it on too thickly, 'I think I need to sleep right now. And then perhaps I'll have a balanced meal later on.'

'Well, just make sure you do. Upton's not on again until half-seven, so you'll need to keep your strength up. If you're lucky I might just bring you some sausages for your tea. I know you like your sausages . . . You've had an ordeal, George. You're still traumatized. Remember?'

George gave a tight-lipped smile and nodded, before disappearing into his room. He closed the door and secured the latch.

He sat down on the bed. Serena had never said a truer word. He was traumatized, yes, but not for the reason she imagined. It was because he had failed in his task. He'd tried to do the decent thing after Judy's death, but all he'd got was imprisonment in a home for the terminally annoying, and it was getting worse every day. But there was more to it than that. The Devil was residing somewhere in the building. He was sure of it.

The only answer was to get back to safety. And that meant one thing: Thade Street.

He lay back on his bed and stared up at the off-white patch of plaster directly above him. He'd come to know it only too well over the past couple of weeks. Not surprisingly, it was the blankest and bleakest of canvases. There weren't even any signs of wear and tear to inspire intrigue, and the comparatively exciting view of the built-in sixty-watt halogen ceiling light was just out of eyeshot. Even the odd thump from upstairs offered nothing. All of which would have been fine if only he could sleep. But as he lay there all he could see were June's eyes staring down at him. Or, at least, the dark little stones that passed for her eyes.

They were the same eyes as the woman who'd helped to drag him from the Thames that dreadful night, barely alive, shaking and shivering. He remembered her peering down at him on the bankside, a thin man frowning beside her, surrounded by loud and urgent voices. The moon was just behind her head, and she looked as if she had a halo. George had asked her if he was finally in Heaven. She smiled and shook her head. 'Not if we can help it,' she said. Clearly, it wasn't a halo at all.

He was drifting now. He could see other faces around him. Figures nodding and clucking like Middle Englanders at a hanging, their white coats luminous against the dull-blue nylon curtains drawn around his bed. One of them, a scrawny man with dark reptilian eyes and a half-hearted smile, was leaning forward and speaking to him as if he were a small child. 'You're very lucky, you know,' he said, carefully enunciating each syllable as he fidgeted with his clipboard. 'You'll live to see another day.'

George scowled at the man. He was too close for comfort. He could see thick black hairs like insect legs poking out of his nostrils.

'You must be very glad to see me,' said the man, his smile now curdling to a sneer. He was wrong, of course.

George tried to move, but he felt dizzy. There were wires coming out of his arms and chest connected to bags of fluid on poles and big grey machines on portable tables. It looked like a scene from one of the hospital dramas he'd seen on television.

'Please try not to move,' said the man, narrowing his lizard eyes. 'My name is Dr Mara. Do you remember yours?'

George peered up at the man's waxen face, flanked by tufts above his temples. His eyelids were like crêpe paper, and his sharp nose was wreathed with spindly rose-red veins. George knew he'd seen him before, but he didn't know where.

Clutching his clipboard like a shield, the man leant forward and tried again. 'Now I have to tell you that you've been badly injured. Do you remember what happened to you?'

George could feel Mara's warm, gamey breath on his cheek. He tried to look the other way, but he couldn't. So he stared up at the pale face as it drifted in and out of focus. The features seemed to be changing. The nose was sharpening to a point, while the eyes were turning black as coals.

'You're no doctor,' slurred George, half asleep. 'I know who you are. Heaven knows how you've lied to me . . .'

Mara stood up and turned to his colleagues, scratching his bald head in a mock gesture. 'Hmm. Apparently, I'm not a doctor. Well, what am I doing here then?'

They all smiled and gave sniffy little laughs.

'Now then,' said Mara, looking down at him again. 'I'll ask you once more. Do you know how you got here?'

'No,' mumbled George.

'Well, do you have any family? Any brothers or sisters?'

'I have amnesia,' said George. 'That's all I can remember . . .'

George opened his eyes. He was back in his room at Bayview. He blinked the sleep away, and for once the flawless off-white ceiling seemed reassuring.

There was a loud thump on the wall, followed by what sounded like something crashing to the floor next door. He hauled himself up on to his elbows and looked at the clock. It was ten past six.

He could hear shouting now.

There was another crash, followed by a loud cry and then, a few moments later, the inevitable knocking at the door.

'Are you in there, old man?' It was Perry. He knocked again.

'Yes . . . Just having a nap,' said George.

'Well, can you open up, old boy? Sorry to disturb you, but I need your help rather urgently.'

George sighed as he reluctantly got off the bed and made his way to the door. He undid the latch and slowly opened it to be greeted by Perry holding up a newspaper. 'Can I have a P please, Bob?' he said.

George looked at him with bleary eyes. 'So what's the problem, then?'

'Need your help with the old crossie,' said Perry, brushing past George and heading for the chair by the window. 'I need a four-letter word beginning with J. Nasty piece of work. Summer month . . . Any ideas?'

'June,' said George, closing the door.

Perry sat down, then pointed his pen at him and winked. 'Got it in one. Not a fan. And now for the real crossword. Six letters. Irritable. Begins with T and ends with Y.'

'Is this another joke?' sighed George. 'Because I was planning to have a bath and take my pills.' It was at times like this that Perry pretended to be deaf. 'You said you needed my help urgently.'

Perry looked up from his newspaper. 'Indeed I do. What would happen if the recycling men saw an unfinished broadsheet crossword in the rubbish bin? If the middle classes can't even finish the crossword they might think there's a chance for rebellion. I'm only trying to keep the peace . . . It's got a T in the middle, by the way.'

'Tetchy. And now I'm afraid I really must go to the bathroom.'

'Well, don't let me stop you if you're good to go, old boy,' said Perry. 'And, by the way, is that clock right?'

'Yes, I think so.'

'Well, what's it doing in Bayview, then?' said Perry, winking.

George sighed and went into the tiny bathroom.

'Perhaps you could ponder Welsh market town while you're in there,' said Perry. 'Eleven letters. Got a B and a G in it.'

As George bent towards the sink he could hear more noises next door. He put his ear to the wall. There was definitely someone in Perry's room. He ran the tap for a moment, pretended to fart loudly several times, coughed and came back into the room with an obvious gait. 'Did you hear that?' he said, frowning.

'Yes. And you might want to take something for it.'

'No, I meant the thumping next door.'

Perry looked up from his paper. 'What thumping?'

Suddenly, as if on cue, there was another noise from the neighbouring room. It sounded like someone dropping something then shouting. Perry sat bolt upright in his chair. 'God in Heaven, what's that?'

'Well, I think you ought to find out. I thought it was you when I heard it before.'

Perry shook his head. 'No. I've been downstairs all afternoon . . . I tried to get rid of it, but it obviously didn't work. It's back again, and I don't know what to do. I'm not even sure whether it's safe to go in there any more. You see, George, whatever it is . . . well, it's obviously trying to hurt me . . . I need your help.'

'OK,' sighed George. 'I'll see what I can do. But now, if you don't mind, I must rest. You can't confront the Other Side with flat batteries, you know. We'll take action after Upton's performance this evening. I promise. Why don't you go back downstairs now, and I'll see you in the Palm Lounge later on.'

Perry nodded and offered George his hand. 'I don't know how to thank you, old boy. You're just the man. They don't like it up 'em . . .'

'Don't panic,' said George as he showed Perry the door. 'Oh, and it's Abergavenny, by the way.'

Perry looked baffled.

'Welsh market town,' said George. 'Eleven letters.'

7

RETURN TO SENDER

It was time to get wise, and there was no time like the present. George knew that he had to leave Bayview once and for all, and Upton Silver's evening performance presented the perfect opportunity.

It was beginning to get dark outside now, and Upton would be on again soon. George drew the curtains and turned on the bedside lamp. It was subtler than the ruthless halogen ceiling light, which obliterated any shadows. The curtains made the usual scraping sound as he pulled them along the rail, and for a moment he felt like kneeling below the window in case anyone was looking. It felt as if something was lurking in his memory, right at the very back of his mind.

George put on his coat and looked around the room for the last time. He could still hear the noises next door. But there were voices now, too, laughing and goading, and he couldn't help thinking that they were directed at him.

He'd arrived at Bayview with nothing, not even a name, but he'd managed to collect a few possessions over the last couple of weeks. And it was these, carefully secured in plastic carrier bags, that he now placed in the tartan wheelie bag Serena had given him. She had called it 'a gift from an admirer' but wouldn't say more than that.

There was a knock at the door.

'Special delivery service,' said a voice.

George felt a wave of panic. 'Is that you, Tom?'

'Er, no,' said the voice.

He was confused. 'Well, what sort of delivery is it?'

'Why, it's your favourite, of course,' said the voice.

He quickly took off his coat and wheeled the tartan bag into the bathroom before clearing his throat and opening the door.

It was Serena. She was smiling broadly and holding a tray. On it was a plateful of sausages with a dollop of mashed potato and some cutlery.

'I knew you wouldn't have made yourself any tea,' said Serena. 'So I thought I'd bring you your favourites.'

'I don't know how to thank you,' said George, slyly blocking the doorway and trying to take the tray from her.

'No, no,' said Serena, pushing past. 'Let me take it. It's heavier than you think.' She took the tray through and placed it on the small table beside the window. 'Now do make sure you eat them before they get cold.'

'You can be sure of that,' said George, reluctantly sitting down.

Serena paused for a moment and looked around the room. 'Have you had a sneaky spring clear-out, Mr P?'

'No . . . Why?' he asked nervously as he tentatively began his meal.

'Well, it just looks a bit bare, that's all.'

'You know I'm a tidy chap. But let's not talk about that. Let me say thank you for these delicious sausages.'

'And what's your coat doing on the bed?'

'D'y'know, I remember having sausages like these at the seaside,' he continued, desperately trying to change the subject.

'It was chilly, and the sausages warmed me up no end. I remember there were lots of people laughing at me. I can see their faces now as vividly as I can see yours. That always used to happen to me . . . It was always very cold beside the sea.'

'Do you like the seaside, then?'

'Oh yes, very much,' said George, chewing. 'Almost as much as I like these lovely sausages.'

'Well, why don't you come on the day trip we're planning to Brighton?'

'Er, will you be you going, too?'

'Of course. I wouldn't miss it for the world. It would do you a lot of good, you know, to get away from it all.'

George choked slightly on his sausage. 'I couldn't agree more. I'll certainly think about it . . . Oh, these really are delicious, Serena. Thank you. I'll finish them all off, and then I think I'll retire for the evening.'

'What? No more Upton?' said Serena. 'Don't let June put you off. She was just in one of her moods. She's the Devil in disguise, you know.'

George nodded uneasily. 'No, it's not June. I just think I need the rest. I'll probably be able to hear him up here anyway.'

'Well, I suppose you shouldn't overdo it. It does seem a shame, though . . . Do let me know if you start feeling unwell or anything.'

'I will. Of course.'

'OK then,' said Serena. 'See you on the other side.' She paused at the door and smiled. 'Sweet dreams, Mr P. And I'm glad you like your sausages.'

It was just after eight-thirty when George finally wheeled the tartan bag out into the corridor. He then quietly clicked his door shut and looked at it for one last time. Fire-retardant plywood stained with teak-effect varnish. Number 22 – a Smith number, a Perrin number, a centred heptagonal Erdős-Woods number. Suffice to say, it was significant.

Nervously he crept towards the lift. Quite why he was being so cautious he couldn't say. Upton was the perfect decoy, yelling 'You ain't nothing but a hound dog' at the top of his voice in the Palm Lounge. And, anyway, nobody would have thought twice about him leaving his room, albeit wearing a coat and dragging a bulging tartan wheelie bag, which was proving to be a lot heavier than he'd anticipated.

He was nervous as he entered the lift and pressed the button for the ground floor. The doors sighed as they closed. There was the usual bump when it reached its destination. It pinged loudly and opened its doors. He winced as he gingerly made his way down the hall towards reception. He could hear them clapping in the Palm Lounge as he worked his way past the notice board towards the empty reception area, staring down at the carpet as he tried to keep his nerve.

So far so good, he thought to himself.

He could hear Upton singing, 'We're caaaaaught in a traaaap . . .'

Suddenly the lift pinged behind him.

'Hello there,' said a voice as it stepped out of the lift.

George tried to ignore it. He was nearly at reception. The window walls and automatic glass door were getting closer by the second.

'Yooohoo,' said the voice, a little more loudly this time. It was getting closer.

George looked around. A white-haired man in a blue suit was standing by the stairs. 'Don't I know you?' said the man. He had a kindly face, which seemed more used to smiling than frowning. The top of his head was completely bald with pure white tufts above his ears. He seemed familiar.

'Are you off out?' asked the man, making his way up the hall towards George. 'Well, do wait for me.'

'Er, no, I'm just taking some things out to the recycling bins,' said George. He pointed at the wheelie bag. 'Had a bit of a clear-out.'

'I'm Horace, by the way,' said the man, offering George his hand. 'How do you do? I was just off out to post a letter.'

George could hear Upton being called back for his first encore. He was starting to panic. 'Well, I can post it for you if you like. I mean, on my way to the recycling bins, of course.'

'That would be most kind of you,' said Horace, fishing in his pocket and bringing out a grubby brown serviette. He offered it to George. 'Would you like a Ritz cracker? My mother always said, "Take something with you for the journey."'

'Oh, thanks, but I'm in a bit of a hurry.'

Horace fished around in his pocket again. This time he handed him a brown envelope. 'Here's the letter. It's a blueprint for one of my inventions.'

'I see,' said George, putting the envelope in his coat pocket. 'So why aren't you in there with Elvis, then?' He gestured towards the Palm Lounge.

Horace grimaced. 'Didn't really fancy it . . . And, anyway, you look like you need some help. I could wheel your bag for you while you open the doors if you like.'

George was suspicious, but he wasn't about to refuse an offer that would speed up his exit from the building – particularly as Upton was now crooning his last. 'Teeeell the folks back home this is the promised laaand calling, and the poooooor boy is on the laaaaaahne.'

The two old men struggled through the glass doors and made their way out on to the dimly lit forecourt. The street-lamps were already on, as were the lights in the windows of the dreary houses opposite. It was colder than expected, but the fresh air was intoxicating, completely free of the vague, ever-present stink of end-of-tether toilets and geriatric dinners.

'Thank you so much for your help, Horace,' said George. He could feel the excitement mounting. He was now only a couple of roads away from the Bartholomew Arms, Edmunds Cut Price Store (apostrophe-free) and other high-street highlights.

'*Ne dankinde*,' said Horace. 'That's Esperanto for "You're welcome."' He smiled at George. 'I could tell you where the recycling bins are, but you don't really want to know, do you?'

George felt a little embarrassed. 'Well . . . as Elvis would say, it's now or never.'

'You have a nice trip now. And do bring me back something nice.'

'I will,' said George, wheeling the tartan bag across the fore-court as swiftly as possible. 'I promise.'

'Oh, and don't forget the letter,' said Horace, waving.

The wheelie bag seemed excessively loud as he trundled it along the pavement, its tartan pattern glowing like a beacon beneath the streetlamps. He was walking as quickly as he could now, which wasn't very fast.

He paused for a moment to look up at the darkening sky. The clouds were gathering around the full moon. He was his own man again, ready to return to Thade Street and restart his life. He could already feel his spirits rising. He even felt a jig coming on, or at least an involuntary rubbing of the hands, but perhaps now wasn't really the time or the place.

The side-roads were comatose, and the high street offered

no surprises. All the usual street species were present. Broken-spirited drunks touring the benches, hooded youths walking as if they'd got rickets and halfwits marching blindly on as they stared down at their mobile phones.

He was beginning to struggle with the wheelie bag. It really was much heavier than he'd anticipated – which was why he was now perched on a low wall in front of Edmunds Cut Price Store (no apostrophe). A dog had decided to sit beside him. So far the two of them had been offered money three times by passers-by. George had always thought the world a painful place full of selfish people, but perhaps he was wrong. Or perhaps it was merely the public's obsession with dogs. That or the glare of the streetlamp above him.

He began to feel a deep sadness at the thought of having to leave it all behind him one day. Of course, he'd make visits like the countless apparitions that he'd encountered throughout his life, but it would only be like looking through a window. He put his head in his hands. He was tired and cold. The jig had long gone, and all he could hear now were the howling sirens and the grey-green river lapping over the stony beach.

Suddenly a small van pulled up beside him.

'Yo,' said a young man, rolling down the window. 'You is from da home, yeah?'

George squinted at the headlamps.

'You look all shook up, bro,' said the young man as the driver got out of the van.

George suddenly came to. He could see a picture of Elvis in a rhinestone suit on the side of the van. Available for parties, weddings and bar mitzvahs.

'Ah, Mr Silver,' he said. 'My good-luck charm.'

'You're that bloke from earlier, in't yer?' said Upton. 'When that woman started shoutin'.' The Deep South twang had gone, leaving only the Cornish brogue.

'I know. Wasn't it terrible? She's quite mad, you know.'

Upton nodded. 'She's the Devil in disguise, boy . . . Mus' say I weren't much lookin' forward to goin' back on stage again this evenin'.'

'Well, I thought you dealt with it very professionally.'

'Thank you,' smiled Upton. 'So where you off to at this time o' night?'

'Er, I'm off to my brother's actually.'

'And where's 'e then? Can we give you a lift?'

George nodded. 'Er . . . Yes, of course. He's in Lambeth. Near the Thames. I can show you.'

'Roight. Well, you'd better hop in then,' said Upton. 'We're passin' that way.'

Karel put the wheelie bag in the back of the van as George climbed aboard. It was a tight squeeze.

'You comfy there, squire?' asked Upton.

George could only bring himself to grunt an affirmative reply. He was wedged in the middle of a seat for three, pressed towards the dashboard with his leg next to the gearstick. Upton coughed. George suddenly felt a damp patch on his cheek.

'I'll probably be touchin' your leg quite a lot,' said Upton, pulling out and speeding down the road. He pointed to the young man. 'This is Karel, by the way.'

'That's a nice name,' said George. 'Er, isn't it usually . . .'

'Naaaah, bro,' said Karel, staring down at his phone.

'It's a different spelling, this one,' said Upton. 'Got a K and an E.'

'Well, my name's George, so there's no confusion there.'

'Seriously doe, dere's no confusion with Karel neeeeva,

yeah?' said Karel, still staring down at his phone. George grunted and nodded, then suddenly remembered the letter Horace had given him. He took it out of his pocket and looked at it.

'Dat for ya bruv, is it?' said Karel.

'Er, no. It's a letter, and I need to post it. It's very important.'

'Well, you'll have to get a proper address on it first,' said Upton. George looked at the three words Horace had written on the envelope: 'London Patent Office'.

'No such number, no such zone,' said Upton.

'Oh dear,' said George. 'I must have forgotten to put it on there. I'll deliver it by hand tomorrow when I've visited my mother in Lambeth. Borough of . . .'

There was an awkward silence.

'Ah fink you meant bruv, bro, not muvva,' said Karel.

George forced a laugh. 'Oops, sorry. Don't know what's wrong with me.'

Karel turned on the stereo, and Elvis crooned from the speakers.

Upton gave a loud sigh. 'Karel. You know the rules. Not after. Only before.'

Karel retuned. 'Sorry, granddad.'

'Good Lord. Who you calling granddad, then?' laughed George, trying to break the tension.

'Er, mah granddaaad?' said Karel.

'Yup,' said Upton. 'I know I don't look old enough, but I am actually his granddad. I weren't lyin' when I said I was born in 1947. You just weren't listenin', were you?'

'Well, I had that evil June in my ear. Remember?'

There was a pause as some vacuous pop music suddenly filled the van.

'Is that what they call pop music nowadays?' said George, trying to make conversation. 'It's not a patch on Mr Silver, is it? What do you think, Karel?'

'Er . . . is me actually,' said Karel. 'Is mah demo. Ah made it.'

George swallowed hard. 'Well, I didn't mean I didn't like it. I meant it was . . . better, really. It all used to be a bit basic in my day . . . I mean, we've moved on since Elvis Presley, haven't we . . . ?' He tailed off.

Karel turned off the music. 'So, how often d'you visit yer bruvva, den?' he asked, staring down at his mobile again.

'Oh, you know. Whenever I can.'

'Let you aaat, den, do dey?'

'Well, it's not a prison,' laughed George. 'Not yet anyway.'

'I s'pose not,' said Upton. 'That would make me Johnny Cash . . .'

George gazed out at the streets as they passed. They were all starting to look the same, as if he'd seen them all before. As the van turned into a quiet road George felt a horror slowly creeping over him.

'I'm sorry, George,' said Upton. 'But we 'ad to check. It was only roight. Karel's been sending texts to Serena.'

They pulled up on the forecourt.

'She said to bring you back, bro,' said Karel.

George looked at the sign next to the manicured bushes: 'Bayview Retirement Home – Putting Care First'. Serena was standing beside it ready to greet them, and she wasn't smiling. He could feel his heart sinking through his shoes and down into the drains. There really was no escape.

Karel helped George out of the van and gave him back his wheelie bag.

'Be seein' you,' said Upton. 'And good luck with the letter.'

He paused and looked at George for a moment. 'Have you ever been to Brighton?'

'Of course,' said George.

Upton smiled briefly. 'I just wondered if you remembered ever going there . . . to the end of the pier, I mean . . .'

George nodded and forced a smile. 'Anyway, thanks for the lift,' he said, waving Upton goodbye.

Serena led him silently back across the forecourt.

'Thought I'd just go for a small trip,' said George. 'You said it would do me good to get away. Change is as good as a rest and all that . . . I just thought it might bring me out of my shell.'

Serena paused and pointed to a sign on one of the glass doors. It read 'All Dogs Must Be Kept On a Lead'. But to George it said 'Go Ask, Upton Dealt Me Bad Sell'.

She sighed as they entered reception. 'Please go upstairs, George,' she said. 'I'll talk to you tomorrow.'

George sat in his room with his palms pressed against his eyes. It may as well have been a prison cell. Or perhaps the Other Place. It was all-out war now. He remembered Judy's words and thought of something he loved, and this time it helped.

Perhaps Judy would visit him now. He knew she was angry with him, which must have been why she wasn't making an appearance. But she would soon forgive him, surely. He'd tried to get away after all, and he would try again soon. He would never give up. Never.

He opened the curtains and looked out at the full moon, safely up in the heavens and shrouded in mist, shedding its light over the pie-chart garden. Or should that be the shared grounds. The communal area. The rotting green. The park for the aged.

He started singing softly to himself: 'Be it ever so humble, there's no place like home . . .'

8

YOU AIN'T SEEN NOTHING YET

It was late morning, and George was sitting quietly in the Palm Lounge discreetly trying to draw attention to the fact that he was sitting quietly in the Palm Lounge. He was alone except for June, who was perched on her chair in the corner, vividly made up like a pastel drawing and staring into the middle distance as per usual.

He'd been trying to toe the line since his Upton outing. That had been a few days ago, and he was now convinced that he'd made it back into Serena's good books – or, at least that's how it seemed. After all, as she'd explained, it wasn't actually a crime to leave the building; the staff just needed to know where everyone was. 'We have a duty to others,' she'd informed him, although she wouldn't actually say who those elusive 'others' were.

He was sitting at the laminated reading-table, next to the double-glazed windows, pretending to read one of the geriatric tabloids. Serena had propped open the french doors, and he could feel a breeze on his back. Gone were the dull stink of defeat and the musty smell of cheap and cheerless furnishings; the room was now being treated to the heady scent of the outside world. It was a breath of fresh air in all senses, and if it hadn't been for June the Gargoyle moping in the corner with her headscarf like a bandage he might even have felt a rare pang of happiness. Or, at least, a fleeting sense of peace.

He put the much-fingered copy of *Silver Citizen* back on to the table, alongside yesterday's papers complete with abandoned crosswords. Then he sat and watched a warm patch of sunlight as it trawled the industrial carpet like a radar. Soon it would mount one of the high-backed chairs and slowly climb the plasterboard wall. This was about as exciting as it got in the Palm Lounge.

June cleared her throat as if she were about to speak. Thankfully she wasn't. According to Serena she always brought her own breakfast down from her room, hence the large plate on her lap that was now accommodating something that looked like a bun. George watched her slyly as she slowly took a bite. Chewing is never attractive, but June took it to another level, snarling at the food before jamming it into her mouth. Her jaw moved sideways as well as up and down as the saliva dissolved the carbohydrates, before sending what was left of the bun down her ancient oesophagus to a grisly end, doomed to drown in her dyspeptic stomach's acid slurry.

It was then that she started picking her teeth with her little finger, opening her mouth wide and forcing it inside, all the way to the back, right up to the liver-stained knuckle. She reminded George of the old woman who walked up and down the street where he lived when he was a boy just after the war. He could see her now, plump and waddling as she walked, sidling up to him with her thin red smile and ovoid chin, saying something at random then springing back as if she'd been startled. She'd then freeze with a look of mock anger on her face, the steel-grey hair that hung about her jowls shifting like weeds in the wind, before suddenly bursting into hideous laughter. She thought she was being funny, but she was just being frightening.

George had made the mistake of catching June's eye, and she was now staring at him, seemingly without blinking. His only defence was to grab a Sunday supplement at random and pretend to read it. He could feel her hard brown eyes on him as he scanned the paper's PR-driven bilge. She cleared her throat again, more loudly this time. For one joyous moment it sounded as if she was about to choke to death.

'Bloody man,' she growled, pointing to the ceiling with an antique finger. 'Always making noises.'

George couldn't help looking up from his paper. 'Er . . . what sort of noises?' he asked.

'Bang bang . . . THUMP,' said June, hitting the chair arm with her fist for added emphasis. George rustled his paper in self-defence. He was beginning to feel uneasy. With her stony eyes and unforgiving stare, it was if she was casting a spell on him. 'Bang bang . . . THUMP,' she said again, hitting the chair even harder this time.

He flinched as he felt a hand on his shoulder. He could feel his heart beginning to race.

'Nice to see you, to see you nice,' said a voice behind him. 'Only me, old boy. Came in via the garden. Lovely day out there.' It was Perry.

'You nearly gave me a heart attack,' said George, as Perry pulled out a chair and sat down at the table.

'Taken aback, eh?' tutted Perry. 'Well, now you know what I have to put up with on a daily basis.' He looked at George. 'It's tough living in the Overlook Hotel.'

'What are you talking about?' asked George. His initial urge to lunge across the pool of papers with fists flying had been dulled by the realization that he was now, at least, no longer alone with June.

'I'm talking about my haunted room,' continued Perry, leafing through the copy of *Silver Citizen*. 'The one you said you'd help me with the other day before making a dash for it.'

George cleared his throat and retreated to his newspaper.

Perry seemed genuinely tense. 'The power of Christ compels you,' he said, a little too aggressively. 'I'm telling you, George . . . I don't know how much more of it I can take. It never stops. Bang bang . . . THUMP,' he said, hitting the table with his fist for added emphasis. The breeze from the french doors suddenly seemed stronger than before. It was now shifting the pages of one of the papers on the table.

'I said I'd help you, and so I will. But in the meantime would you be kind enough to close the doors? It's getting a bit chilly in here.'

'They're already closed, old boy,' said Perry. 'I closed them when I came in. Habit, I'm afraid.'

Bernard entered the room with Clarissa close behind. George hated himself for it, but he was almost pleased to see them. It felt as if a parachute had opened for him at the last minute as he plunged towards the dull earth, albeit so that he could land back in hell.

Clarissa looked tired. 'Did anyone hear that funny noise this morning?' she asked, making her way to one of the armchairs. 'I thought it was a seagull . . . Bloody car alarm.'

'I really must apologize for my friend,' said Bernard with fake formality. He'd only been in the lounge for a minute and was already starting to be annoying.

'Who you calling a friend?' scoffed Clarissa. 'Wanting to

rummage around in my oversized pants doesn't make you a friend. It makes you a stalker.'

'Well, you know what they say, Clarrie,' said Bernard, rummaging through the papers on the laminated table. 'Any love is good lovin'.'

'Wasn't that Billie Holiday?' asked Perry.

'She sounds like she had a good time,' said Clarissa, still looking for a chair.

'Heroin, poor thing,' said Bernard, leafing through a broadsheet.

'She certainly was,' said Clarissa.

'No, I mean the drug. That's what killed her,' said Bernard.

Clarissa stopped in her tracks. 'Well, it wouldn't have been a heroine that killed her,' she barked, pointing her finger. 'It would have been a jealous coward. And, anyway, I meant the holiday bit.'

'Oh, I give up,' said Bernard, flinging the broadsheet on to the table.

'Temper, temper,' said Clarissa, lowering herself into a high-backed chair. 'Oh, I do like your outfit, Georgie.'

'Thank you,' said George, feeling slightly self-conscious. Today he was sporting a bright-purple jumper with beige trousers, along with the red-striped trainers. Mercifully his luminous underpants weren't visible.

'Well, come on then,' said Clarissa. 'Entertain me, somebody.'

Bernard turned on the television and began flicking through the channels before settling on an old sitcom.

'Oh, I know this fella,' said Clarissa, pointing at the screen. 'He's a right bloody shit. I wouldn't go to his shop. Would you?'

'But it's *Open All Hours*,' said Bernard.

Clarissa's face froze for a moment in a look of mock anger. 'I don't care when it's open. He's got a moustache, and I hate moustaches.' She suddenly burst into a fit of fake laughter.

'Shame,' said Bernard. 'I was thinking of growing one.'

'Well, you don't want to look like him, do you? Or that Nazi bloke. I'd stick to growing your vegetables if I were you.'

'Better shave mine off, then,' said Perry, stroking his facial hair. 'Fought against the blighter. Certainly don't want to look like him.'

'I'm talking about bloody Ronnie whotsit,' said Clarissa. 'He's on the television.'

'It's Barker,' said Bernard. 'There are two Ronnies. One small, one big. Barker's the big one.'

'I hate dogs,' growled June in the corner. 'Especially big ones.' There was the customary silence. 'I'm allergic. They make me cough.'

'Well, big or small, he's still a bell end,' said Clarissa. 'Or, as *he* would say, a b-b-b-bell end.'

'That's not how he talked in real life, you know,' said Bernard. 'He's just playing a character.'

'And how would you know?' hissed Clarissa.

'Because it's a TV comedy series,' said Bernard. 'And I was an actor, remember?'

'Is that why you dye your hair?' asked George.

'To die, to sleep, to sleep, perchance to dream . . .' said Bernard.

'Lovely jubbly,' said Perry.

Clarissa sighed and shook her head. 'But you weren't actually in anything . . .'

'Yes I was,' said Bernard, haughtily. '*Some Mothers Do 'Ave 'Em*. Mike Crawford. Lovely fella. I played Second Man in Hat.'

'Oooh, Betty,' said Perry, unable to resist.

'Fine,' said Clarissa. 'But that doesn't stop Ronnie whotsit being a stuttering little shit, does it?'

'A big shit,' said Bernard. 'A stuttering *big* shit.'

Clarissa winced. 'Oh, stop it with your big shits . . . I had trouble down there this morning. It's a funny old business, this medication. Can't get used to it. Sticking things up your behind. I don't care if it does stop me soiling myself. Why can't I swallow it like normal pills? It's anathema, that's what it is.'

'Oh, you don't want one of those,' said Bernard.

'Look. Can we talk about something else, please?' said Perry, taking a paper bag from his jacket pocket. 'I'm just about to eat a muffin.'

There was a sudden burst of canned laughter from the television.

'I don't know why they're all laughing,' scowled Clarissa. 'It's not bloody funny, is it?'

'Well, change the channel then,' said Perry.

'Don't bother,' sighed Clarissa. 'You'll only end up with a fake documentary about youths wearing jewellery and baseball caps and breaking into cars.'

'I wouldn't blame them,' said George. 'I hate cars.'

'It's not the cars, it's the wankers who drive them,' said Clarissa. 'Especially the big posh ones. Big cars equal small genitalia. That's the rule.'

'Well, there must be a gardening programme on somewhere, eh, Bernie?' said Perry, trying to change the subject.

'Oh, don't worry on my account,' said Bernard. 'I'm not a great TV watcher. I just appear on it. Although I do indeed maintain a corner of a foreign field, as you have observed. Courgettes and tomatoes mostly. Organic, obviously.'

'Oh God, you really couldn't be more of a prick if you tried, could you?' sighed Clarissa. 'You'll be running out of Earl Gay tea next or ordering a fuckaccino. I don't know how much more of this I can take.' She got up and made her way to the french doors. 'Christ. *He's* there being a prick, *he's* over there saying he fought in the war when he didn't and *he's* sitting there dressed like a fruit.' She stared out at the communal garden. 'Honestly, if you want to get old quickly just come and live in one of these bloody places. I mean, just look at that bloody tree. I know every leaf on that bloody tree. Makes me sad just to look at it.'

'Well, I dread to think how you're going to feel in the autumn then,' said Bernard, turning off the television.

'They're not my friends, you fruitcake,' said Clarissa. 'They're leaves.' She walked slowly back to her chair.

'Actually, I quite fancy some fruitcake,' said Bernard.

'Well, if we sit here long enough I'm sure we'll probably get some,' said Perry.

'If we sit here long enough, matey,' snarled Clarissa, sitting down, 'we'll all be dead. I mean, what are we? Little children waiting for Mummy to bring us some snacks. Ooh, look, Mummy, I've shit myself. Help me wipe my arse.' She took a deep breath and sat down. There was an awkward silence. 'I'm bloody trapped in here! All I did was get old. You start with bars on your cot, and you end up with childproof locks on your bloody windows. Sitting, ticking with the clock and watching your toenails thickening.'

'Sounds like one of Bernard's poems,' said Perry.

'Oh, please don't start him off,' said Clarissa.

'And, anyway, you can't like life too much', said Perry, 'or you'll never want to leave.'

Bernard sat down in the chair beside Clarissa and put his hand on hers. 'Well . . . why don't you try to get out more, then?'

'What? And hang around with all those dickheads who visit museums?' She sniffed and took a tissue out from her sleeve. 'All they do is complain about the bloody cruise they've just been on.' She blew her nose. 'It's been bloody years since I went on holiday. I've got more chance now of going to the moon. All I do now is sit in this bloody place all day staring at the curtains or the television, not caring which is which.'

'Well, why don't I take you to a gallery, then?' ventured Bernard.

'I've tried going to galleries,' said Clarissa. 'But I always end up looking at the frames. They're more interesting than the pictures. Then you get one of those audio guides, and you walk around looking like you're flying a helicopter.'

'Well, how about the British Museum, then?' said Bernard.

'Went there once. Just lots of statues. All looked like that Mr Bean fella.'

'What about the library?'

She blew her nose again. 'Libraries give me the creeps. All the whispers by the shelves and the peeping around corners. It's worse than this place. Full of weirdos with carrier bags breaking wind in the biography section, going from literary criticism to stage and screen without a by-your-leave . . . And, anyway, most of the books are covered in bogeys. And now they've got computers in there as well . . .' She stopped and took another deep breath. 'Maybe I'll just jump on my whotsit and never come back.'

There was a pause.

'What whotsit?' said George, looking up from his Sunday supplement.

'My Sprinter Deluxe,' said Clarissa. 'I'm going to take it on our trip down to Brighton.'

'Ah, yes,' said George, suddenly interested. 'I really must sign up for that trip.'

'Well, I wouldn't get too excited, old boy,' smirked Bernard. 'The coach was full, last I heard.'

'Well, he can squeeze in next to me, then,' said Clarissa. 'Or how about sitting on my lap?'

'I don't know what you want one of those silly scooters for anyway,' said a disgruntled Bernard. 'What's wrong with a good old walking-stick?'

'It's better than a stick, you prick,' said Clarissa. 'You can't put your bloody shopping on a stick, and you can't drive around on the pavement getting on everybody's nerves.'

'I must say,' said George, putting down his newspaper, 'it sounds like it was Heaven sent.'

Clarissa stood up from her high-backed chair. 'Well, you can have a look if you like. Fancy a quick one?'

'I certainly do,' said George, almost smiling.

Drawing found in Room 22,
Bayview Retirement Home

'Blitz Doll', dated January 1968

9

YOU'VE GOT A FRIEND

'Come on then,' said Clarissa as she and George made their way along the hall to the deserted reception area. 'Never mind that bloody Bernard. Let me take you to see *Chitty Chitty Bang Bang*.'

They paused briefly by the notice board as Clarissa pressed the exit button. The thick glass doors slid apart with a hum and released them both into the wild, otherwise known as the forecourt, where all plant life had been drained of character by too much care and attention. George could see a large brown dog lying patiently by the gate. It sat up when it saw him.

'I used to have a dog just like that,' said Clarissa. 'Carole she was called, with an "e". Had her when I was a little girl.' She seemed to wilt a little. 'Always scratching and banging her back legs she was. Bang bang . . . THUMP. Woke the whole bloody house every morning. Like clockwork. Loved her, though. If I close my eyes I can still see her. Better not do that when I'm on my whotsit.'

George looked at the dog. It seemed eager to play, but when he slapped his thigh in a welcoming gesture it was reluctant to advance.

'Well, come on, then,' said Clarissa, grabbing George's sleeve. 'Let's visit the communal car park. I mean, it doesn't get much more exciting than that, does it?'

She led George slowly across the Tarmac to what looked like an outsized hunchback in a grey cloak squatting beside a minibus. 'Here it is.' She carefully removed the grey rain cover to reveal what now looked like a giant toy, a chair screwed to a scooter, its metallic yellow base glinting in the spring sunshine. 'You know, I'm really not sure if I'm ever going to use it . . . That's the problem.'

'But how did you get it?' asked George, suddenly riddled with envy.

'Had to spend my pension on something, didn't I? Mind you, they don't let you have one until you've been here for a while. Cars are for wankers, so I didn't want one of those. And, anyway, I can't even drive.'

George was now fondling one of the armrests. 'Well, what about driving this? Is it easy?'

'No bloody idea. I've never ridden it. Probably never will.'

'But I thought you were taking it to Brighton?'

Clarissa sighed. 'I am. I'll probably dump it there in the sea. I mean, can you honestly see me on a Sprinter Deluxe? I just wouldn't feel confident. It would be one big embarrassment. Like eating a banana in Soho. I suppose I could take it to the pound shop and cruise around the aisles. At least then if I crashed into the shelves it wouldn't cost me much.' Clarissa sighed and stroked the scooter's handlebars. Tears began to appear in her eyes. 'It's all too late, really . . . Nothing's going right at the moment. There's just too much to learn. They make you watch one of those videos before they let you anywhere near it. And you can't have a CB radio either. It probably makes a terrible noise, too, like that bloody little shit who careers around on his motorbike screaming up and down the road in the early hours of the morning. Have you heard him?'

George shook his head. 'Well, perhaps I could try sitting in it,' he said, taking hold of one of the handlebars. 'I just want to see how it feels.'

Clarissa frowned. 'But it might start automatically. Then we'd be stuck. It's got direct drive transaxles and a detachable basket. You can try it out in Brighton. On the seafront. And that's a promise.'

George smiled and ran his hand up and down the fake leather seat.

'Morning,' said a voice near by. It was Serena, looking slightly harassed. 'Planning another great escape, are you, George? Just came to say that there's tea in the Palm Lounge if you're interested.'

'Is there room on the coach for His Majesty when we go to Brighton?' asked Clarissa.

'Indeed. His Majesty is most welcome,' said Serena, before heading for the forecourt. 'Now do come on in for tea.'

'Looks like you won't be sitting on my lap after all,' said Clarissa as she and George made their way back to the entrance.

'That'll be one in the eye for Bernard,' said George, stopping briefly to look at the big brown dog at the gate. It was standing now, not sitting, and it didn't seem so friendly. George could see its hackles rising as he stared.

The glass doors to reception slid open and they went back inside. The deserted entrance hall seemed darker than usual after the spring sunshine, as if the sky had suddenly filled with grey rain-laden clouds.

'I do hope they find that poor little dog,' said Clarissa.

'What dog?' asked George.

'The one on the notice board,' sighed Clarissa. 'I told you

when we were coming out just now. It was like the dog I had when I was a girl.'

'I thought you meant the dog at the gate,' said George.

Clarissa looked at him. 'Coo-ee!' she said, waving her hand in his face. 'Anyone in there? There's no dog at the bloody gate . . . Forget to take our pills this morning, did we?'

'I don't know,' said George, pausing at the bottom of the stairs. 'Perhaps I did. Better go up and take them now . . . I'll see you later in the lounge.'

George kept thinking of the big brown dog as he made his way to his room. The corridor was ripe, as ever, with the familiar stink of meaty meals and troubled toilets, and it was a relief to reach the door to his room. As he put the key in the lock there was a loud thump from Perry's side. He felt a sudden coldness like the old north wind as he opened the door. It wasn't helped by the note lying on the mat. He picked it up. 'WELCOME BACK! THAT'S THE WAY TO DO IT!' it read in capital letters. It didn't say who it was from.

George closed his eyes and sighed. 'Are you there, Tom?' he said. He waited a few moments. He always closed his eyes when inviting Tom to appear. He didn't like seeing his vaporous form materialize out of nothing, starting with a hand or even the head, until it finally resembled the little boy he knew so well. Seemingly solid yet non-existent. Ethereal and not real. He always felt a profound sadness, which, he knew deep down, repaid him for the events on the bombsite all those years ago.

'Morning,' said a little voice. It was Tom. 'You all right, pops?' All George ever had to do was say Tom's name and he'd appear.

'Not really,' said George, opening his eyes. 'I think I'm being watched.'

'By who?'

'It's whom.'

'And who's Hoom?'

'Never mind.'

There was another thump on the wall. 'Is it him next door?' asked Tom. 'He's a bit of a scaredy cat. Won't leave that room of his, although he says he wants to leave it more than anything.' Little Tom shivered.

'What do you mean?'

'I mean it's a real shame,' continued Tom, looking up at George. 'We could have some great laughs, we could, but he says he just can't leave.'

'Why not?'

'He says the whole place might blow up.'

George sighed. 'You don't mean Perry, then?'

Tom shook his head.

'Well it sounds like you've got a little friend in there. A kindred spirit, so to speak.'

'But he's attached, pops. He can't leave. He needs to be freed.'

'No he doesn't. He can walk out whenever he wants to. He's in charge. Nobody else. Tell him that when you see him next.'

Suddenly there was a knock at the door. There was always a knock at the door. It's what Bayview doors were for. They were instruments of psychological torture via raps on fire-retardant hardboard.

'Hello. Are you in there, Mr P?' said a voice. 'It's Serena. Can I come in? I've got a special something for you.'

George opened the door. Serena stood there awkwardly in the corridor holding a package. 'I have a special delivery for you, Mr P. May I come in?'

Tom ran across the room and hid behind the chair.

'Yes, please do,' said George, waving his hand and stepping aside, grateful for a dose of normality.

She seemed a little nervous and unusually formal as she walked across the room and sat down in the chair beside the window. Her silken nurse's uniform seemed to glint in the spring sunshine. Even when settled into the chair she remained perched upright with her knees together and the special package placed primly on her lap. Perhaps she could sense Tom, who was now standing shyly beside her.

'I promise you, Mr P,' said Serena, tapping the package gently, 'this will really cap it all.'

'And how do you know it's a "special delivery"?' asked George, reluctantly approaching the chair.

'I just do,' she said, handing him the package. 'It's from someone you know.'

George took it and placed it carefully on the sideboard near by. It was lighter than it looked. He suddenly felt uncomfortable.

'Well, aren't you going to open it then?'

'Er, no, not yet,' said George, standing awkwardly in the middle of the room.

Serena seemed a little disappointed. 'That's a shame,' she said. 'I was curious to see what you thought of it. I think it'll . . . inspire your imagination.'

'Well, I'll definitely tell you about it later on. It's just that I'm feeling a little tired all of a sudden.'

Serena sighed and stood up. She looked out of the window for a moment. 'My, it's a lovely day out there. I always feel a bit guilty on days like this. They're just too nice to be wasted.'

Tom was still beside her, and he was now looking up at her with awe. Slowly he reached out to touch her, but as he did so she walked away, and the little boy was left stranded beside the chair.

'Well,' said Serena, making her way to the door. 'I do hope the package is of interest.' She paused for a moment. 'You know, Mr P, you really are a stubborn old man sometimes.'

'I know,' said George. 'It's my trademark. And what do you mean, *sometimes*? Thank you for bringing me the parcel.'

'Are you remembering to take your medication?' asked Serena, as George ushered her out of the room.

George nodded and smiled, then closed the door behind her, reluctantly savouring the heady mix of her perfume and the lingering stench from the corridor.

Tom was still standing by the chair, although now he was looking out of the window. George walked over to him. He seemed sad. It was moments like this when George regretted not being able to put his arms around him.

'I don't think she knew that you were there, Tom,' said George. 'That's why she walked away.' Tom nodded reluctantly. 'Let's open the package together, shall we?' said George. 'Then I'll help your friend next door to leave the premises. I promise.'

George looked at the package on the sideboard. It was a bulging padded envelope. A sickly yellow. He went over and picked it up, shaking it gently. Something was tinkling inside. He looked at the printed address label: 'For the attention of Mr P (Room 22)'. There was writing on the back: 'I'M CLOSER THAN YOU THINK!' it said in capital letters. The note put through his door had also been in capitals. He looked at the words and felt tears gathering in his eyes. The voodoo was obviously working. Reluctantly he began tearing at the top of the envelope. Then slowly, like a conjuror, he pulled out a long piece of striped material from the top of the package. There was a handwritten note with it. It read: 'The sun has got his hat on. Have you?'

George examined his gift. It was a silken cap with red-and-white stripes and a small silver bell on the end.

'That's the way to do it!' said Tom excitedly. 'I'm going to go and tell the boy next door about your hat!' He waved goodbye and disappeared into the ether.

George took a deep breath and opened the window. He looked out at the forecourt. The big brown dog had gone now. He stood there for a while, feeling the breeze on his face and listening to the birds. He could feel the hat in his hand. It was silken to the touch, with the little bell tinkling whenever he moved. Slowly he put it on his head.

He felt transported to another place. The spring day in north London was fading fast, and all he could see now was Judy by the Thames. They were walking together very early one Christmas morning, leaning into the wind. She was holding on to her bonnet beside the railings that marked the end of one world and the beginning of another. Thin black waves broke on the pebbled beach and rasped over the stones. The wind thudded in his ears as they linked arms. She immediately pressed herself to him, and they walked for a while like competitors in a three-legged race. She was carrying a package that George had given her, and the wind was tugging at the wrapping like a child. She was trying to open it secretly as they walked.

'No, don't open it now, Judy,' said George.

'But I'm impatient. I want to see what my darling boy has given to me.'

George smiled. Judy had always been his weak spot. 'Well, then. At the very least, please allow Mr P to shelter you from the wind as you unwrap your present.'

They stopped walking, and George opened his greatcoat, wrapping it around them both.

She tore open the paper and looked at what was inside. 'Gloves! Why, Mr P, that is the very thing I wanted.' Very carefully she slid one on to her right hand, easing inside it little by little, splaying her fingers as she pulled it down towards her wrist. She then held it up to him. It was a perfect fit. 'Did you buy them at the Burlington Arcade in Piccadilly?'

'No,' he said, somewhat sadly. 'I made them myself.' He could see her fingers were already stretching the crude, zigzagging stitches at the edges.

She looked surprised. 'Well, I certainly couldn't tell, Mr P.' Then she very carefully put on the other glove and held both hands up to her nose. 'Mmm. Fish skin, if I'm not mistaken.' The scales twinkled in the sunlight.

'Do you like them, Judy?' asked George

'Very much,' she said. 'Yes, I like them very much indeed. Thank you, my darling Mr P.'

The Thames had gone now, along with Judy and her fish-skin gloves, and George was back at Bayview. He sat down in the chair. He could feel the sun on his face. It was making him squint. He'd do anything to see her again. Anything. He'd tried calling out her name, but no one had come running.

The one thing he knew he had to do right now, though, was to get out of this room. The walls, thumps and all, were starting to close in again.

He could hear Perry's muffled yells next door. No words, just primeval grunts and shouts. He'd have to go next door to see what he could do – with Tom's help, of course. If only to stop the constant noise.

10

KNOCKIN' ON HEAVEN'S DOOR

George stood outside Perry's room gathering his thoughts. He'd taken off the striped hat with the bell on the end and stuck it in a drawer. He was now clutching two pens, which would double as a makeshift crucifix, plus a mug of 'holy water' – half tap, half urine. He knocked on the door. The hall now smelt of mildew, which was better than the usual food-driven fetor. He could hear Perry on the other side, mumbling to himself and undoing the latch. After a few moments the door opened a few inches and Perry's leering face appeared. 'Heeere's Georgie,' he said, before finally waving him into the room. 'I knew you wouldn't desert me, old boy.'

'At your service, sir,' said George.

'Lovely jubbly,' said Perry, miming firing a gun. He seemed very tense.

George stopped and looked around the room. 'So what exactly seems to be the trouble?'

Perry sighed. 'Well, by all accounts, George, we seem to have an overenthusiastic magazine fan on our hands. A poltergeist with a fixation on *Railway Modeller*. Particularly the early and now rare issues.'

'Have you tried telling this entity to pick on more recent editions?' asked George.

'No. Hadn't thought of that,' said Perry, studying the mug and pens in George's hand. 'I see you've come prepared. Looks like a fine white vintage wine in there.'

George offered him the mug. 'Please feel free to try some. It's holy water.'

'Er, smells a little fruity if I'm honest,' said Perry, grimacing and waving the mug away.

George paused to look around the room in fake solemnity. It was stuffed full of paraphernalia. If it wasn't in a glass cabinet it was framed in a box on the wall or on a shelf or spilling out from under the bed. Model cars, planes and trains, small plastic figures, magazines and more magazines.

'Lots of kit, I think you'll agree, eh, George?'

'Definitely plenty to throw around . . .' said George, spying an official-looking badge on the mantelpiece.

'Aha, well spotted.' Perry went over to the mantelpiece and took the badge in his hand. 'I used to be a community police officer, you know. I keep this badge. Can't use it any more. Just a souvenir. That's the worrying thing, really. So far magazines seem to be the favourites to throw around, but all of these other treasures – as you can see – are at risk, too. And I wouldn't want to get in the way of one of these things flying across the room.'

George nodded sagely. 'Well, let's see what we can do then.'

He placed the mug of watered-down urine on a shelf near by, then adopted a theatrical pose with his hands, touching the tip of each thumb to the tip of each index finger. 'This is the *guyan mudra* position,' he said, standing in the middle of the room. 'It brings calm and opens doors. The index finger is Jupiter, and the thumb is the ego.'

Perry nodded sheepishly and backed away into a corner.

After a few moments George took the two pens from his

pocket and held them aloft. 'Biros,' he said, taking a deep breath and pretending to close his eyes. 'Now, please be silent.' He was actually squinting at the window to keep his balance as he held up the crucifix pens. After a while he spoke. 'Hmm,' he said in a numb voice, 'I'm getting something . . . Magazines. Glossy pictures, yes. Old ones, too.'

'*Railway Modelling Monthly* by any chance?' ventured Perry from his corner.

'Yes. That's the one. Rails. Wheels . . .'

'*Steam Railway*? That's monthly, too.'

'Yes, yes, *Steam Railway*. It's all coming to me . . . Chug, chug. You like throwing things, don't you? Clickety-clack. Oh yes. Throwing things . . .' George held the pens aloft now and slowly made the shape of a cross.

'Goodness. You've done this before, haven't you?'

'Mmm.' George raised his hand in another theatrical gesture. 'I can definitely feel a presence . . . Do you like model trains and railways? Well, do you? Yes? Aha, well, throwing is bad. No more magazine throwing, please.'

All it needed was another couple of minutes of this pantomime, followed by some incantations. 'You must stop it. Stop it now, I say . . . Now go to the light. The light, I say . . .'

'Ooh, I'm coming over all tingly,' said Perry. 'That's the spirit, eh?'

'Now is not the time for bad jokes,' said George, as an aside. 'Unless, of course, you want it to start on the glass cabinets. Demons thrive on bad jokes.'

George opened his eyes and solemnly put down the pens, then he held up the mug of odorous unholy water to the window. It was slightly warm. 'Be gone,' he said, tipping the mug and pouring some of the diluted urine over the carpet.

'Steady on, old chap. I only had that cleaned last month.'

'It's only a few drops,' said George. 'It'll work wonders. I can feel a presence all over here. A child . . . A boy. Yes, a boy. Be gone, boy!'

Perry fell silent.

'I know you are here in this room,' said George, pausing for effect. 'Am I right? Knock once for yes and twice for no.' There was a loud knock. Perry jumped. 'Thank you, Tom,' said George under his breath.

Knock, knock. Bang bang . . . THUMP.

'Er, I said knock once for yes . . .' said George.

Two more knocks followed.

George cleared his throat. The room was now unusually cold, and he was beginning to feel uneasy.

'Tom?' he said. His voice was faltering. 'Is that you?'

Suddenly one of the curtains was drawn swiftly along the rail. George put down the mug of unholy water and picked up the pens. 'Be gone,' he said, nervously holding them up to the curtains in the shape of a cross.

'What's happening, George?' asked Perry.

'Keep calm. Tom, we need some help here.'

George could feel his skin tingling. He was looking at the silhouette of a small figure standing in the doorway of the windowless bathroom. It was dark, almost too dark to see, but it was definitely the profile of a young boy. He couldn't see his face, but he could see that he had dark hair and that he was wearing shorts held up by little braces.

George could feel his heart thumping as he slowly approached the child. He knelt down a few feet away. 'Hello, little one,' said George. 'Do you know Tom? Is he your friend?'

The boy stood there stock-still.

'Do you know where little Tom is?' asked George, peering into the darkness.

There was a long pause before the boy finally nodded.

'Er, who are you talking to?' said Perry.

'Shh, please,' said George. He moved a little closer to the boy, who backed away into the darkness. 'Are you OK? Do you want to tell me anything?'

'Oh, for Heaven's sake,' said Perry.

'Look, will you please be quiet for just one bloody minute,' said George angrily. He looked at the boy and pretended to shoot Perry with a gun. He couldn't see the boy's face, but he heard a small laugh.

'I saw that,' said Perry. 'I'll put it down to demonic possession.'

The boy now took a step forward into the room. He was still obscured, but George could see that he was pointing at the badge on the mantelpiece. Suddenly the other curtain began to close, with the room becoming darker by the second, as if a long black cloud was filling up the sky.

'Turn the light on, Perry,' barked George. 'Do it now!'

'I'm trying,' said Perry, pressing the light switch. 'But it just won't work.'

There was a loud thump. Then another. Bang bang . . . THUMP. It sounded like something was falling down the stairs. George stood up and tried turning on the light. Perry was right. Nothing worked. He tried a table lamp, but it was no use.

'I've had enough of this,' said Perry, marching over to the curtains and pulling them open again.

George looked around. The little boy had disappeared. He felt a sudden wave of sadness, mixed with guilt.

Perry looked pale as he stood there by the window, as if he

was about to pass out. 'Look, old boy, I'm suddenly beginning to feel a bit off . . . I can't thank you enough, but I think you should go now.' He put his hand on George's back. 'Honestly, old man. You've gone beyond the call of duty.'

'OK,' said George, taking his mug of unholy water from the table. 'I'll go. But just let me finish the job.' He moved to the middle of the room, clutching the mug and the biros. 'Be gone,' he cried as if on stage, suddenly dropping the mug of diluted urine, pretending it had been wrenched out of his hand.

'Bloody hell, George,' said Perry. 'It stinks!' He was right. It did. And it would stain, too.

George feigned faint horror as if witnessing a vision. 'Message for Perry. Get out of this dump. It's doing you no good!'

Perry was now standing by the door. The fun was over.

'I'd really like you to leave now, George, if you would. I'll never forget what you've done here. Do please let me know how I can return the favour.'

George walked to the door. He could smell the mildew from the corridor, and he could still hear the boy's laugh in his head.

'I'll let you know if I need any more help,' said Perry. 'Brighton here we come, eh? Nice to see you, to see you nice.' Perry all but pushed George out into the corridor and closed the door behind him.

George stood there alone out in the hall, clutching the empty mug and the crucifix biros.

He put his ear to Perry's door. For a while it was silent, then he heard him talking out loud. 'Leave me alone,' he was saying. 'It wasn't my fault. There was nothing I could do. For God's sake, leave me alone, will you?'

George felt disturbed as he unlocked his door and entered

his room. Who was the little boy? And where the hell was Tom? He almost regretted pouring the unholy water all over the carpet.

The room was dark as he went inside. It should have been bright, but the curtains were closed. The weak little patches of daylight spilling out at either end of the window were the only sources of light. He stood there for a few moments, beginning to feel weak. Instinctively he slowly knelt to the floor, just as he had done in Perry's room. For some reason, kneeling always seemed to bring back memories. He could hear hysterical voices now beyond the curtains, as if a crowd were out on the forecourt. The sound seemed so familiar. He could hear a drum roll, too, followed by the crash of a cymbal.

George was haunted by memories wherever he went. The Brighton trip would be fun, but it would be laden with thoughts of going there as a child, staying in a hotel with leaded windows. He remembered the lounge, filled with imported palms like clustered knives, with a sad-looking woman who sang into the evening for a fee. Cutlery clanking and plates as big as wheels. Out on the promenade there was a chill wind feeling up the market stalls, with traders bundled up against the cold like Captain Scott, short on change and itching for a sale. A sea of faces pushing past. He could already smell the fish and chips and the rain in the air and the man with the pan in the van serving sausages on serviettes.

Every tiny thing referred to something else in George's mind; the longer you live, the more complex living becomes. The older you get, the more there is to recollect. He'd always been cursed by the ability to recall scenes in vivid detail. It was why he'd started drawing. That rush of thoughts, too copious to keep inside his head. And if it wasn't drawing it was humming.

This went through three phases: first, realization that he was doing it; second, embarrassment; third, not caring. All it took was a sound or a smell to take him back, as if a spell had been cast. Broken only when the so-called real world managed to press its way back into his consciousness. It wasn't that he disliked the memories – indeed, he thrived on them – it was just that there were too many of them.

All he could think of now, though, was the shy boy in the room next door hiding in the shadows. He'd always seen ghosts, ever since he was a child. From an early age he had complained tearfully of the 'coldness' that the 'other children' brought to his playroom. 'Seeing the gallery and not just the picture' was what his mother used to call it. 'Ghosts are ten a penny,' she'd say, waving the problem away with her hand. 'They grope you as they pass, without so much as a by your leave.' George, though, had always been troubled by the apparitions that his mother seemed to take in her stride.

He stood up. His back felt stiff, as always. 'Tom? Are you there?'

The room was silent. There was no sign of the boy anywhere.

George closed his eyes. In a moment he was back on the bombsite where Tom had met his end, strewn with weed-ridden rubble, pale and dusty like an old western . . . He'd never quite come to terms with the guilt he felt about Tom's untimely death. The two of them used to pass the ruined church together on a daily basis, and every time they did George promised little Tom that one day he'd be able to have a look inside. So when the council were about to pull it down and build a housing estate in its place, as was still common in the early 1970s, he let little Tom sneak inside.

It was a simple, everyday decision, but one he would regret for the rest of his life. As George stood staring at the broken altar, Tom slipped and banged his head. His skull cracked with a sickening thump as it hit the rubble. George ran out into the street and screamed for help. Then he went back in and tried to move the body. He wept like never before as he stared down at the dark inky blood seeping out on to the pale stone. Help arrived by chance, in the form of a retired ambulance man, but it was all too late.

At first Tom came back to haunt him as a spirit full of rage, tormenting him and throwing things like a poltergeist, whispering half-formed words and growling in his ears like the wind. He remembered the first night it happened. It was only a few days after the accident.

He'd been woken by thunder in the middle of the night, like demonic drums, and for some reason he felt drawn to get up and look out of the window. The sky grumbled as he looked out at the trees, like mascara brushes in the moonlight. He could hear a child's voice in one of the gardens.

It was cold. He went back to bed. The rain rattled on the window as he lay there curled up like a question mark. He could hear footfalls now near by. He did not dare close his eyes for fear of what he might see, and yet he couldn't bring himself to look.

A few nights later, though, there was a breakthrough. Driven to the edge by the nightly visits, George screamed back at the noises in his ears. He railed and screeched before sinking to his knees exhausted.

Gradually, over the next few nights, a shadow began to visit him. It was the boy's spirit this time, not the over-emotional earthbound entity that had formed around his anger. It seemed even more scared than George, taking refuge in the corners of the room, knowing neither where it was nor how it had got there. Then slowly, one night, out of the darkness, the shadow came forth. It was the faintest outline at first, stepping forward cautiously as if expecting to be punished.

But George could only love him. And he had done so ever since.

Drawing found in Room 22,
Bayview Retirement Home

'Tom Closing His Eyes', undated

11

RAINING IN MY HEART

George could already hear the Brightonauts chattering loudly outside on the forecourt. No words, just a prickly dirge punctuated by the occasional bout of spiteful laughter, presumably at someone else's expense. The last trip they'd taken had been to West Wittering. He went over to the window. There they all were, lining up like schoolchildren; ready to board the coach that would inevitably be 'too hot' or 'too cold' or 'too bumpy', with the driver, likewise, 'too timid' or, simultaneously, 'taking too many risks'. The sun was out, and the sky was blue. It was so bright, in fact, that George was having to squint as he looked out. But that made no difference to the Bayview inmates. Most of them were wearing coats, and some were even sporting gloves despite the relatively balmy spring temperatures. After all, there was a definite 'chill in the air', the weather being 'not like it used to be – I mean you never know when it's going to turn nowadays'.

George was tired. He'd been woken at dawn by a series of farts – not the usual parp but more of a bubbling sound; not so much curt as squeezy. They'd sounded as if they were accompanied by some sort of matter, solid or otherwise. But he didn't want to check, so he lay there listening to the waking world with the stench locked under the blanket.

He finally got up when Serena knocked to remind him that there was a place for him on the coach. Luckily the farts were all bark and no bite. So he'd packed his bag and dressed hastily, donning the usual red-striped trainers, plus a pale-green satin shirt that looked like a blouse and a pair of crimson flared trousers, finally covering it all up with a grey coat.

It would surely be a lovely day, and yet he couldn't help feeling strangely apprehensive about the trip, which was why he left the room with a heavy heart, locking the door behind him. He would use this trip to regain his confidence after the Upton episode. Then he would leave Bayview and go back to Thade Street.

'Hi-de-hi, campers,' said a voice at the end of the corridor. It was Perry. 'You're not planning another getaway, are you, old buddy?' He eyed up George's bag as he made his way towards him.

'That wasn't an escape attempt. I was just getting a lift to the shops.'

'If you say so,' said Perry with a smile. He winked and gestured towards his room. 'Job well done, by the way. No more ghosts. Just a very stinky carpet. What the hell was in that holy water?'

George shrugged. 'At least the weatherman says it's clear today,' he said, trying to change the subject. 'I think we'd better go downstairs.'

It seemed like a long journey to the forecourt.

'Bit chilly out here,' said an old man in an anorak. 'This weather's not like it used to be in my day. I mean, you never know when it's going to turn nowadays.'

'It's spring, you div,' sniffed Clarissa, who was wearing her trademark red cardigan. 'What do you expect?' She stood there watching as her mobility scooter was placed carefully in the luggage hold.

'Listen, everyone,' said Serena, who was standing close by. 'In case any of you are wondering why Clarissa has been allowed to take her mobility scooter on the coach, it's because it's brand new and she wants to christen it officially on the seafront.'

'Going to break a bottle of champagne on it, is she?' said Bernard, who had suddenly appeared, wearing a white short-sleeved shirt and a handkerchief on his head.

'What you talking about?' barked Clarissa. 'Georgie boy here is going to piss all over it. Aren't you, Georgie boy?'

'That's the spirit, eh, George?' said Perry, climbing aboard the coach. 'A spot of good old seaside humour to get you in the mood.'

'Do you think I should I dress up in leather for my Shoprider?' asked Clarissa.

'Er, no,' said Serena. 'I think it'll be fine. Although a crash helmet might be a good idea.'

'It certainly would,' said George. 'For everyone else, that is.'

Once the doors were all closed the coach began slowly manoeuvring its way out of the forecourt like an old blind elephant. The journey down to the coast was the bit that George had been dreading most, particularly as he was trapped in the window seat next to Perry. Still, at least June, the embodiment of misery, wasn't on board. He wondered if she even knew about the trip.

'So, no more happenings then?' he ventured awkwardly as the coach grumbled its way out along the sparsely populated high street.

'Nope,' said Perry. 'Like I said, job well done.'

There was now a distance between them. If George had known that a mock exorcism would have had this effect, he'd have been round there banishing spirits at the very first opportunity.

Perry cleared his throat. 'Seen anything good on the TV lately?'

'Not really. Just a documentary about railways and trains. Hidden stories, apparently. You know, secrets.'

Perry sighed. 'Look, George,' he said, adopting a hushed tone that was difficult to hear above the general mêlée. 'I have no idea what you're getting at. Now, please can we change the subject?'

There was a pause as both weighed up their next move.

'Well, what would you like to talk about, then?' asked George.

'The fact that we're going to have a lovely day out, perhaps?'

George was silent. He couldn't think of anything to say on the subject.

For a while they both looked out of the window and watched the houses go by.

'You see things that you want to forget when you're a community police officer,' said Perry after a while. He held his hands out in front of him and flexed the stump of his ring finger. 'You never stop wondering whether you could have done more . . .'

'Excuse me,' said a voice behind them. 'Do you think the driver knows the way to Brighton?' George looked around. It was a woman standing up in her seat.

'I hope so,' said George.

'Good,' said the woman. 'Because he'd better not ask me. I've got no idea.'

'I'm sure it'll be fine,' said Perry. The woman seemed relieved and lowered herself back into her seat. Perry looked at the row in front. Clarissa was there, sitting next to Bernard.

'So what do you think of Clarrie's scooter then, eh, George?' said Perry, loudly. 'Fine machine, eh? Too good for the likes of Clarrie, though, don't you think? I reckon you've got your eye on it, haven't you, George?'

Clarissa poked her face between the seats. 'Oh yes, he's desperate to ride my apparatus. Aren't you, Georgie boy?'

'Indeed I am,' said George so that Bernard would hear. 'I can't think of anything more pleasurable.'

Silence and a fake nap had killed any attempt at conversation by the time they had hit the dual carriageway, and George was now sitting watching the countryside flash by. Cows pinned to the flitting fields. Sheep pylon sheep pylon sheep. Brighton twenty-two miles. Slowdown sign. Roadworks. The trees passing swiftly as if on a conveyor belt. Conspiring firs. Needle spires. Brighton seven miles. Delays likely. B&Bs with crumbling porches, sumptuous Georgian houses with too many rooms.

The sky had clouded over the further south they'd gone, and it was now thick and grey, like hostel pillows. Drops of drizzle like tiny scratches were starting to appear on the window as they entered the outskirts of Brighton. The coach eventually drew up along the seafront. The driver spoke into a microphone. 'Good morning, everyone. As you can see, we're by the sea – yes, I know that rhymes – so I thought it would be nice to start with a little promenade along the front. Perhaps we can go to the pier.'

Bernard put his hand up, like a child in a classroom.

'Er, yes?'

'Excuse me, but technically that's not actually a rhyme,' he said. 'It's actually the same word but spelt differently. I know because I'm a poet.'

'Aha, well spotted, the man – sorry – the poet at the back. Anyway, as I was saying, perhaps we can go to the pier a little later when we'll be having some lunch. So, who's ready for a little perambulation?'

There was silence.

'Why don't you just bog off?' said Clarissa.

'I'm sorry?' replied the driver.

'I said –'

'Er, yes,' said Bernard hurriedly. 'She said, why don't you just log off? You know, like you do with a computer. You must be tired. You've done a lot of driving.'

'No I didn't. I said *bog* off,' said Clarissa.

'Well, I'm sure there'll be toilets along the front somewhere,' said the driver.

The coach was silent for a moment.

'OK, everyone,' said Serena, lolloping awkwardly between the seats as she moved towards the front of the coach. 'Now, you all know the details of where we're going to meet later. You can walk along the front or even on to the pier, but do bear in mind that wherever you go there will always be a carer near by.' There were frowns from the seats. 'OK,' said Serena, trying to sound enthusiastic. 'Now, let's make for the seaside!'

Suddenly it was slow-motion mayhem as dozens of old people prepared to leave the coach.

George was standing beside the railings next to the beach. They were thick and antiquated like his fellow travellers. He was watching the sea unfold. There was a coldness about the place. Aside from the never-ending chill of the wind and the now grey sky, it felt bleak. The sighing sea was more glum than calm, pocked and gruel-grey. The seagulls suddenly enormous as they landed out of nowhere. Strutting haughtily one minute, then cowering and taking flight the next. Shitting when they could and hovering above the tourists as they ate their lukewarm fish and chips. It was not how he'd remembered it.

He looked around. Just beyond the coach, huddled in the arches beneath the built-up road to Rottingdean, was a parade of overstocked souvenir shops and snack bars. The plastic tables and chairs were empty. White wire stands were stacked with buckling postcards. Five for a pound. T-shirts and fridge magnets and miniature models of Brighton Pier. Now the happier memories of coming to the seaside with his mother started flooding back. Sitting at sticky tables in dusty B&Bs and sweaty cafés, with grey cups full of builders' tea. Bliss. It was always just the two of them, and she did her best to be cheery. It must have been hard for her, whatever the weather.

He could hear voices now as the ocean rolled in. The same stuttering hysteria that he'd heard when he was getting ready in his room at Bayview. He closed his eyes for a moment. A sea of open mouths and pointing fingers were suddenly before him. Whenever he heard people shouting and laughing, his instinct was to hide, to duck down behind a wall. But there was no wall. He turned around. Clarissa and Bernard were approaching, bickering as usual.

'Well, I never used to go on holiday, actually,' Bernard was saying. 'It wasn't worth it. You have to tell everyone about it when you get back, over and over. How was your holiday? Fine. How was your holiday? Fine. And so on.'

'Well, I only remember going there the once. Sick as a dog, I was. Shitting through the eye of a needle. Couldn't smile without something popping out. Stank, too. Like a corpse. Bloody Blackpool.'

Suddenly they were beside him. Bernard had his arm loosely around Clarissa. She was frowning. 'Honestly,' she said. 'You come all this way and all you bloody hear is cars. Where's the sea? You can't even smell it. It's just doughnuts and fish and chips. And look at all the seagulls making the place untidy . . .'

'At least the weather's cheered up a little bit,' said Bernard, winking.

'It may as well be raining as far I'm concerned.'

Bernard sighed. 'Do you ever stop complaining?'

'That's not complaining. That's telling it like it is. And the wind is hurting my ears. It's a gale. I mean they go on about this global warming, but I'm all for it. I don't remember it being as bad as this in my day.'

'But that's the point about global warming . . .'

Perry approached. Somehow he'd managed to don shorts.

'Is it really warm enough for those, old boy?' enquired Bernard.

'Well, what about your short sleeves?' huffed Perry, briefly standing on tiptoes.

'But I have a jumper at hand. Shorts seem a little . . . brave.'

'Careful. Nothing withers on the vine,' said Clarissa.

'Look, when you've been through a war like I have,' said Perry, 'a little wind shifting around your shins is bearable.'

'Well, I suppose you were wearing shorts in the war,' said Clarissa. 'It's what little boys did . . . But why the socks?'

'A man's got to have socks,' said Perry. 'I'd say why the hand-kerchief on the head, eh, Bernie?'

'It's a reference to T.S. Eliot.'

'Oh, why don't you just piss off,' said Clarissa, unlinking arms and going to stand next to George. 'Come on, George, let's be off to the pier.'

'That's what they call "pier pressure", George,' said Bernard.

They all began walking, as if powered by their pointless conversation.

'I was definitely wearing shorts in the Blitz,' continued Bernard, undaunted. 'We weren't evacuated. Oh no. My mother and father said we'd be safer with them, so we stayed.'

'Shame you didn't get bombed,' observed Clarissa.

'Those bombsites were every boy's dream playground,' continued Bernard. 'Very dangerous, mind. I remember a wall falling down when my friend Billy tried to climb it. Bloody nearly fatal. Poor sod broke his ankle.'

George suddenly stopped in his tracks and yelled. 'Owwww!' he cried, clutching his leg. (Desperate times called for desperate measures.)

'War wound, George?' enquired Perry.

'No. Just cramp actually.'

'Well, you don't need to tell me about war wounds.'

'He wasn't,' said Clarissa. 'He said it was cramp.'

'Look, why don't you all just go on ahead,' said George.

'Bet you wish you could hop on old Clarrie's scooter now, eh?' tutted Bernard. 'Better watch where you're going, though, when you do. Don't want to end up like my mate Graham Hill. Grand Prix driver. Died in a crash.'

'Shame you weren't with him,' said Clarissa, as a woman ran by wearing tight gymwear. 'Bet you wish you could hop on her, don't you, Bernie boy? Little stirrings in your Y-fronts, eh? Like a mole in his hole having a bad dream.' Bernard looked embarrassed. 'Still, at least you're keeping it to yourself. Saw this man on the bus once. Top deck, right at the front, fiddling about downstairs.'

'I thought you said he was upstairs,' said Perry.

'No, I mean "downstairs".' She made a face. 'Finally came to an end at Tufnell Park. Or at least, that's when he stopped. Got off at Camden. I was quite relieved. Not as much as he was, obviously.'

They were approaching a stone ramp that led down to the beach. 'Well, I think I'll see you later then,' said Bernard, making his way down the ramp. 'Just going to see if the sea's still there.'

Perry now hurried after Bernard. 'Wait! I fancy a bit of a paddle, too.'

'What are you talking about?' snapped Clarissa. 'Of course it's still there. Don't you think you'd have heard about it on the news?'

'It was Dylan Thomas,' said Bernard.

'Oh, you utter prick. I hope you drown.'

'You said it,' said George as he watched them crunch their way across the stony beach. He was now stranded with Clarissa.

Two down, one to go.

12

A WHITER SHADE OF PALE

'I'm definitely not bringing my mobility scooter here,' said Clarissa as she and George entered the Palace Pier's dated metal gateway. 'It'd judder to buggery. Put your bloody back out it would.'

'I'm sure it must have suspension,' said George, not really listening.

'Well, do let me know when you try it out later on.'

'Yes, madam,' sighed George as he looked down at the tired old planks beneath their feet. The sea was visible between each plank, a constant reminder that certain death was loitering below. The whole construction felt like the skeleton of an old liner, beached and beset by sightseers. Infested with ice-cream parlours with plastic cornets for signs and poky little shops selling souvenirs and pick 'n' mix sweets, with a gloomy fairground at the end – the last stop before the heaving grey-green sea.

Clarissa stopped walking for a moment.

'Catching your breath, are you?' asked George, catching his breath.

'No, just looking at this thing,' she said, pointing to a board outside a café depicting a cartoon couple in ornate wedding outfits, flanked by dogs dressed as bridesmaids. There were holes where their heads should have been so that people could poke their faces through and take 'funny' photos. 'Odd place to have a wedding reception. I mean, supposing something priceless got blown into the sea. You'd never see it again, would you? Or if somebody had a tray full of drinks and got blind drunk, then fell over the side . . .'

There was music spilling out from the café. 'Fancy a fandango?' said George, trying to counter Clarissa's hopelessness.

'I think I'll skip it, thanks' she said, studying the holes in the board. 'Do you think I should poke my face through? Now that would be a funny photograph. A cartoon character full of the joys of spring with the face of an old bag.' She walked over to the railings and looked out to sea, squinting as the wind shifted her white hair. It was meant to be a poignant moment, but her words were lost, drowned out by the noise of the amusement hall further up the pier, filled with clunking glamour and robot thieves, souped-up one-arm bandits ready to scour your pockets. All fair chances banned from the building and dumped beneath, amid the copious metal struts and pent-up sea.

George walked over to the railings and stood beside Clarissa. He could hear the seagulls squawking above him.

'Listen to those bloody seagulls,' said Clarissa. 'They sound like that clown fellow. You know, that puppet. The one you looked like when you came into the lounge for the first time.' She looked at his pale-green satin shirt and crimson flares. 'And you're not too far off him now either.'

'Mr Punch?'

'That's the one. With that wife of his. The one that he hits with a stick. Right wanker. And they show it to children, for goodness' sake. All that bloody violence.'

'But it's a tradition.'

'What is? Beating your wife black and blue?'

'No. Punch and Judy. It's part of the seaside,' said George, not knowing why he was defending it.

'Rubbish. Not nowadays it isn't. Someone should drown the little shit.'

They began slowly walking up the pier. George was now starting to feel a little strange. Almost seasick. He wasn't sure what was wrong. All he knew was that the closer he got to the amusement arcade, the more he was beginning to panic.

The arcade felt claustrophobic as soon as they entered it. The purpose of the stately Victorian building, with its intricate glass ceiling and elegant design, had been betrayed by the brash modern interior. George was feeling short of breath now. The room was humming with the same noise level as a factory, crammed with sugar-rush children and bored nostalgic adults, all pumping the machines full of coins. As they crossed the room he could feel the crowds laughing and pointing at him; chanting, too, he was sure of it. He felt like hiding, but there was nowhere to go.

'Why are we coming in here?' George asked above the din.

'Change,' answered Clarissa, pointing to a big fluorescent sign emblazoned with the word 'Change'. 'Apparently it's as good as a rest.'

George frowned. He couldn't hear what she was saying above the din and so dutifully followed her to the mock-Edwardian kiosk, where she reached into her handbag and brought out a white envelope that she placed on the steel counter.

'What can you give me for these?' she asked a lethargic young man sitting behind the glass.

'Well, how much is in there?' replied the man, whose badge said he was called Gary.

'No bloody idea,' said Clarissa. 'Why don't you count them, Gary?'

Gary sheepishly took the envelope and looked inside. He looked at a couple of the coins, then held the envelope up to a colleague in the kiosk. The colleague shook her head and Gary slid the envelope back to Clarissa. 'Where did you get these?' he asked. 'They're not legal tender. I'm sure there are lots of antique shops that might be able to give you something for them, but I'm afraid we can't help you.'

Clarissa sighed and put the white envelope back in her bag. She seemed defeated as she made her way back out on to the pier, with George following close behind. 'Wankers,' she was saying over and over.

They stood by the railings and looked out to sea.

'I've been trying to do something with these coins for years,' said Clarissa. 'For a while, I thought I ought to keep them. Then I realized that it would be best to let them go.' She was looking pale. 'They're not doing me any bloody good.'

'What are they?' asked George, standing a little closer to her so that he could hear her response.

'It doesn't matter. It's all gone now. It's in the past.'

George took a breath as if about to speak, but Clarissa waved her hand at him. There were tears in her eyes. It was turning cold now, and they needed shelter. George could see what looked like a Wild West caravan near by, nuzzled up against the railings with a makeshift stairway attached at one end. It was a bolthole from the noise and the chill sea air. There was a board propped up outside that read 'Get Your Palm Reading Today by Gipsy Tina'.

Clarissa was still in despair. George pointed to the board. 'Why don't you get your palm read? It might just clear the air.'

'Well, it's not the best bloody English, is it?' said Clarissa, looking at the sign. 'And you don't spell gypsy with an "i". She's probably about as gypsy as I am. She's called Tina for a start . . . My palm's unreadable anyway. Too many lines. It's like a crumpled old bit of paper.'

'Well, why don't you try it anyway?' asked a woman behind them with a strong Eastern European accent. 'Perhaps the truth will be plain to see. It is special discount for you today, yes? And maybe I will learn something myself.'

A blonde middle-aged woman in a headdress suddenly appeared before them, gesturing towards the caravan. She was holding a pile of leaflets. 'I am Tina. Perhaps you are my teachers today.'

'Where are you from then?' asked Clarissa.

'I am from this small caravan,' said the woman. 'Where we are from is of no importance. It is where we are going that counts.'

Suddenly a seagull the size of a chicken flew by and almost brushed Clarissa's hair with its wing. Clarissa grabbed George's arm and ducked.

'It's a sign,' said George, shepherding her towards the caravan. 'Come on. At least the seagulls won't be able to attack you in here.'

She reluctantly climbed up the makeshift stairway, fussing her way through the bead curtains and into the small dark interior. It was cramped and smelt of candles, but at least it was warm and away from the brutal racket of the arcade.

'Please make yourself comfortable,' said Gipsy Tina, sitting down at a small round table. 'And when you are ready you can each offer me your hand. Or, if you prefer, I can give you my tarot cards.'

In the half-light her heavily made-up face looked part-clown, part-witch. Clarissa looked at George for support.

'Let go of your fear,' said Tina. 'It is not suiting you.'

There was a candle by a tiny window that looked out on to the sea. George watched its flame fluttering in the breeze.

'I start with the lady,' said Tina. 'Give me your dominant hand.' Clarissa looked confused. 'It is the hand you would hit your husband with . . .'

'What, him?' said Clarissa, looking at George and offering up her right hand.

Tina took it and began studying Clarissa's palm. 'And what is your name, please?'

'Clarissa.'

'This is a very nice name,' said Tina, taking a deep dramatic breath. 'So, Clarissa, please let me now be quiet with your hand . . .'

George sat there with the sea churning beneath them, listening to the sharp cries of the gulls as Gipsy Tina studied Clarissa's palm. He was beginning to feel at home in the twilit caravan. He remembered looking at his father's hands at the breakfast table when he was a boy, with the sunlight glinting on the draining-board near by. Dad would sit there staring at the radio as if it were talking to him, with his hands lying dormant on the tablecloth, as Mum poured the tea and steam rose from the cups. His hands seemed huge and old and marked with experience, even though he would have only been in his late thirties. George was six when his father died, which was when he and his mother moved to Thade Street. After that it always seemed to be raining. He remembered staring out of the window, with the landscape looking like an old film, listening to the rain as it rinsed the gardens and the streets.

Gipsy Tina sighed. 'There is much here, Clarissa. Much.' She looked at George. 'She is a complicated woman, your wife.'

Clarissa looked at George and put the index finger of her free hand to her lips.

'First, let me explain,' said Gipsy Tina. 'You have what we call an air hand. It is hard for you to express emotions. Is this hard for you, Clarissa?'

Clarissa seemed a little embarrassed. 'Well, I've never really thought about it. I mean, emotions are private, aren't they? Not really for public consumption.'

'OK. I am now going to give you two fingers.'

'And the same to you, dear.'

'These are important fingers, your index finger and your ring finger. They are both short. This means that your confidence is not high, and, as I said, you hide your emotions.'

Clarissa was frowning now.

'However,' continued Gipsy Tina, 'these little lumps at the bottom of your fingers are called mounds. And you have a very pronounced one here below your middle finger. It is Saturn's mound. This means a very good sense of duty to your loved ones, which makes up for the emotions you do not express. Is this like you, Clarissa?'

Clarissa took a deep breath. She was suddenly very tense. 'So what you're saying is that I've got stumpy little hands covered in lumps.'

Gipsy Tina looked a little closer at Clarissa's palm. 'There is also something here. A deep sadness. There is a star on your lifeline, which means a shock. You were young. It is a deep mark, and a break here, too . . . You have had deep sadness.'

Clarissa sniffed loudly. George looked at her in the flickering light of the candle. It wasn't the usual sniff, and he could see tears welling up in her eyes.

'Shall I stop now?' asked Gipsy Tina, touching her arm gently.

Clarissa's lips were clamped shut, but she was shaking her head. 'No. Go on,' she said at last, in a faltering voice.

'OK. You will tell me if you want me to stop. I am looking at your relationship lines now, here on the other side. One is long, but one is short and very deep also. This was a short time, but it was also very strong, and it has meant very much to you in your life.'

Clarissa nodded then dropped her head. George instinctively put his arm around her shoulders. She sniffed again and took a tissue out from her sleeve. She was crying now.

Suddenly there was a squawk as a seagull landed right outside the tiny window. Clarissa looked up. 'He sounds like that Mr Punch,' she said, blowing her nose.

Gipsy Tina laughed awkwardly. 'I'm sorry. He is a very loud seagull. He says, "Please, no more for Clarissa."'

Clarissa gently took her hand away.

'Is this OK for you?' asked Gipsy Tina. 'I was going to tell you about the Girdle of Venus . . .'

'That's probably lumpy and stumpy, too,' said Clarissa, getting up. 'Don't worry, it was more than enough, dear.'

'And I shall do you now?' said Tina, looking at George.

He made a face. 'I think I'll come back later. I have terrible rheumatoid arthritis in my hands. Must be the sea air.'

'Well, what about the tarot?' asked Tina.

George shook his head. 'Thank you, but I already know my tarot number.'

'And he's Mr Punch,' said Clarissa. 'Don't want to tangle with that, do you?'

George squirmed.

'Oh well, you must treasure your Judy, Mr Punch,' said Gipsy Tina, taking George's hand. 'She is a good person,' she said, slyly glancing at his palm. She stroked it and smiled. 'Your hands are soft but very stiff. You are sensitive but very stubborn. The truth is plain to see.'

'That's the way to do it!' said Clarissa, wrestling with the bead curtains and stepping out on to the pier. She rummaged around in her bag and gave Gipsy Tina a ten-pound note. 'And you can have this, too, if you like,' she said, fishing around in her bag again and handing her the envelope full of coins.

Tina bowed. 'Thank you. And it is very thoughtful, but I cannot take the envelope.'

'Go on. It's a gift.'

'But I know it is really very precious to you. Please keep it.' She handed Clarissa a business card. 'Thank you. It is the thought that counts. And I hope your hands are better soon, Mr Punch.'

The wind was gathering strength as they walked back along the pier towards the black wrought-iron gates.

'Well, what did you think of Gipsy Tina then?' asked George, a little sheepishly.

'Very sweet,' said Clarissa. 'All that palm stuff, though. It's a load of old rubbish. I was just playing it up so as not to embarrass her.' She was starting to look tired and pale again. 'I think I need some of that Pro-Col, or whatever they call it, to perk me up. I've had enough of this bloody place.'

They paused beside a soft-toy stall. George handed her the business card that Tina had given him. She looked at the words: 'Palms Read Free – Ask Gipsy Tina'.

Clarissa shook her head and walked on. 'She charged me ten bloody pounds!' she fumed.

'It's a good anagram, though,' said George, pursuing her. 'Grand Pier Mask a Past Life, Yes?'

Clarissa stopped and looked back at George. 'Look, if you don't buck your ideas up, dickhead,' she snapped, 'I won't let you have a go on my mobility scooter. You're my bloody guinea-pig, remember? I want to see if it's safe. I don't want to end up like whatsisname draped across a bollard on a traffic island.'

George was baffled. His eyes were open, but they may as well have been closed. It was all beginning to feel like a dream.

'Oh, you know the fellow I'm talking about,' said Clarissa. 'Don't pretend you don't. Poor bugger. He was a good man, and it was all the bloody car's fault. He was cremated, too. I mean, I'd much rather be landfill, wouldn't you?'

'I suppose so. Anything's better than a jam jar full of ashes.'

13

MR BLUE SKY

The sun was shining now and the sky was pale blue as George and Clarissa made their way back along the promenade. She was studying the pavement as she walked. Silent for once, she seemed buried in the past. They both were, but George didn't need Gipsy Tina to kindle his memories. The low-flying plane grumbling along the coastline was already doing that. Suddenly he was a child again, just after the war, running down the road on his way to school. He'd seen smoke at the bottom of the street.

The old house on the corner was on fire. He remembered staring in horror as a face appeared at one of the windows. It was the old woman who used to walk up and down the street all day. She was retching and coughing, trapped behind the glass as thick white smoke gathered behind her. She was yelling for help, screaming and grasping at life like a poltergeist. George could hear a fire bell sounding near by. In desperation the old woman banged on the window with her fist, and the glass shattered, bursting into the stillness of the street and letting loose her screams. 'When are they coming?' she yelled. Terrified, he ran back up the street away from the house as fast as he could.

He came back later that afternoon. The house was a burnt-out wreck. It remained deserted for years. Every time he passed he saw the woman's face at the broken window. He never found out what happened to her.

Clarissa had stopped walking now. A little dog had been following them for a while and was now barking at their heels. 'He's been with us since the pier. I think he's lost, poor little bugger.'

'I know how he feels.'

'No you don't. He's only a puppy.' She bent down to stroke the dog. 'Where have you been hiding then, eh?' she said, scratching its back. 'You know, I'll never forget our dog Carole. My mother murdered her. She used to find piss all over the floor. All over the carpet, everywhere. It was like she had dementia or something. The dog, that is. So my mother had her put down. Turned out it was next-door's cat.'

The little dog jumped up at George. 'I wonder where its owner is,' he said, looking up and down the promenade.

'Right cow, my mother,' continued Clarissa, now absent-mindedly stroking the little dog's head. 'She had that horrible-coloured skin, like the top of a brick. Where it dips. Same colour as a pork scratching.'

George had given up listening. So had the dog.

'Look,' said George, suddenly overwhelmed by her relentless negativity. 'It's a lovely day. Why can't we just talk about something nice for a change?'

'What's the bloody point in that?' she said, getting up and walking off towards the coach. The little dog looked up at George and then scampered away, yapping as it headed down to the beach.

George caught up with Clarissa. She was still in a world of her own, looking down at her feet as she walked. She stopped to look out across the bay. 'It's just that I don't think I've ever really appreciated any of those special moments,' she said, shaking her head. 'I'm just always too bloody clogged up with worry. Couldn't ever see the trees for the wood. Maybe I'm just a stupid cow like my mother.'

'Come on,' said George. 'Let's go and have some fun.'

She looked at him as if he was mad. 'Are you feeling all right?'

He shook his head. 'No, not really.'

They were nearing the coach now. They could see the driver, a rotund man in his middle years. He was standing looking out to sea with his shirt sleeves rolled up and his hands in his pockets.

'Ah, you must be Clarissa,' he said as they approached, adjusting his dark glasses. 'Serena said you'd be back for your Shoprider, or should I say your Go-Get ES5 Ultra Light mobility scooter?' He led them around to the front of the coach where the scooter was parked. 'So did you find the toilet OK, then?'

'What toilet?'

'Well, I assume that's what you meant when you said "bog off" to me before you left.'

'Oh no. I'm so sorry. I actually meant shut up and stop being so bloody patronizing. I suppose I didn't really make that clear, did I?'

'Er, no,' said the driver, hiding his embarrassment by taking out a battered packet of cigarettes from his shirt pocket. 'Well, thanks for clarifying that . . . Or should I say "Clarrie-fying"? I presume you have keys.'

'Indeed I do,' said Clarissa, rooting around in her handbag.

'Well, I'll leave you to it, then,' said the driver, before saluting sarcastically and slipping across the road for a surreptitious smoke.

'Now's your chance, eh, Georgie? Today's the day,' said Clarissa, still rummaging around in her handbag. 'If I can find the bloody keys . . . I forgot to bring the instructions, but the video made it look simple. If you've ridden a motorbike you'll be fine. And it's got non-scuffing tyres.'

'Well, I haven't.'

'You haven't what?' said Clarissa, finally finding the keys.

'I haven't ridden a motorbike.'

The scooter's bright-yellow metallic base glinted in the sunlight, and the warm fake-leather seat seemed to shine.

'Well, it can't be that hard, can it?' said Clarissa, fondling the armrest. George could see she was in a world of her own. 'I mean, it looked easy on the video . . .' She was now talking to herself. 'Go on, you know you want to.'

She unlocked the box behind the seat and put her handbag inside it. 'It's time to seize the moment. That's the way to do it.'

George looked on with a mixture of disappointment and relief as Clarissa slowly climbed on to the scooter and wrestled with the seatbelt. It took a few minutes, and by the time she was secure the drama of the moment had died.

'Did I ever tell you about the scooter I had when I was younger?' she asked.

'I thought you said you'd never had one before.'

'I'm talking about when I was a child, you idiot,' said Clarissa, squinting at the controls and putting the key in the ignition. 'Green it was. Like a big plant. One of those tropical ones with the shoots. I used to call it Doris. No idea why.' She turned the key. The Shoprider made a soft burring sound. 'A proper old scooter it was. Not a bloody trumped-up wheelchair for old biddies like this one.'

The scooter started moving forward, a little more quickly

than she'd anticipated. 'Don't wait up,' said Clarissa, suddenly turning the speed control up to max and heading off along the promenade. George was several yards behind, but he could see that she was gaining confidence, sitting bolt upright and feeling the power in her hands as she hit four miles per hour.

She was shrinking steadily now as she sped off towards the pier, with the sea air on her face and the wind thundering in her ears as the scenery crawled by. This was the day she'd been waiting for. She didn't know why it had taken so long to arrive. How lucky she was to be elderly in the twenty-first century. No more Zimmering around like a cripple with a bar stool. Here she was, breezing along the promenade with her feet firmly on the plastic base, gripping the handlebars as if her life depended on it.

George was hot on her tail, but it was getting harder and harder to keep up. She seemed to be gaining speed, despite the fact that she'd just been overtaken by a group of tourists. He could see her turning around awkwardly in her seat, looking behind her. George waved his arms. There was a litter bin looming ahead of her. He pointed at the bin and yelled. She saw it just in time and swerved to avoid it, narrowly missing a ranting woman with a baby in a buggy. For a terrible moment the scooter teetered on the brink of tipping over as it careered towards the railings. She yanked the handlebars in the opposite direction with all her might. She was back on the straight and narrow again.

George, meanwhile, was still waving his arms. He was advancing now, leaning determinedly into the sea breeze as he strode towards her at full pelt. He looked like a charging rhino, albeit a rheumatic one in slow motion.

But she powered on, like Ben Hur in his chariot, half terrified and half alive with excitement as she glided effortlessly past a toddler and a man with a walking-stick. She then lowered her head and leant towards the handlebars to reduce wind resistance. Everyone seemed to be smiling at her. Except George. He could hear yapping now up ahead. It sounded like the puppy they'd seen earlier.

Clarissa looked around. She could see something out of the corner of her eye moving beside the scooter. But when she looked down at the pavement it was only an airborne fish-and-chip wrapper. With her eyes off the road she suddenly lost control again, veering from one side of the pavement to the other. She was heading for some stone steps now, panicking as she tried to find the brakes. She could still hear the yapping. But where was the puppy?

The steps were getting closer by the second. But so was George. 'Stop!' he yelled. She could see the little dog beside her now. Suddenly it jumped aboard, then up on to her lap as she jerked to a halt at the top of the steps.

She looked at the controls. They were all at zero, including the battery dial.

Suddenly it felt cold again, and rain seemed imminent despite the bright-blue sky. She tried turning the ignition key hopelessly, over and over.

George arrived beside her, heaving for breath. 'I thought you wouldn't make it.'

'Are you all right there?' asked a voice near by. It was Serena. 'That was quite a maiden voyage.'

'I think I've bloody broken it,' said Clarissa, slowly getting off the scooter and wishing for a tsunami. The little dog scarpered down the steps towards the beach, yapping as it went.

'You forgot to charge it up, that's all,' said Serena. 'I'll charge it up for you when we get back.'

'Well, at least I had enough time to check the shitting chassis torque and the handlebar-shaft angle function.'

'I thought you were going to take a tumble down those steps,' said George, still out of breath. 'I was worried.'

'No bloody need. I knew what I was doing, thank you very much. I hate bloody steps at the best of times.'

They heard a grunt near by as an irritable cyclist, dressed in the obligatory garb of an Edwardian circus gymnast, squeezed past.

'Oops,' said Serena. 'I think we're blocking the cycle lane.'

'Bloody cyclists,' moaned Clarissa. 'Dressed up like bloody insects with bodies like sticks. They look like they've just escaped from a laboratory. I mean, it's hardly safer, is it? They should all be beaten to death with their own bikes.'

'And what about Shopriders?' said Serena.

Clarissa ignored her, took her bag from the back of the scooter and slowly began descending the stone steps. 'I'm going to the beach,' she said. 'Anybody coming?'

'Don't mind if I do,' said George.

'OK,' said Serena, turning the scooter around and wheeling it back along the promenade. 'But make sure you're back at the coach by four o'clock.'

'Bloody hard work, these stones,' said Clarissa as they walked down towards the sea.

'I know, but we can't come all this way and not go to the beach.'

They stopped for a moment to admire the view. He could feel a sense of calm coming over him as he watched the heaving sea spill out across the stones before making its rattling retreat.

'This is one of those moments I was talking about,' said Clarissa. There was a pause. She took his arm. 'Will you remember this when we go back, George?'

He nodded. He didn't feel like talking.

'I asked you a question,' said Clarissa after a few moments.

'I know. And I nodded.'

'Well, I hope you do remember it,' sighed Clarissa. 'I will.'

They carried on walking, arm in arm, with the stones crunching beneath their feet. George could hear voices near by. Children cheering, accompanied by a kazoo-like sound. His sense of calm was now retreating like the tide.

'Ooh, look, George,' said Clarissa. She was pointing to a puppet booth beneath the promenade with a small crowd in front of it. 'Let's go and have a look at your friends.'

'Must we?' said George, as Clarissa led the way back up the beach. 'And, for the record, they're not my friends.'

The booth looked as if it had been hastily erected, with its sagging striped canvas shifting in the wind and a tired-looking piece of dark-red velvet hanging down from the small stage like an old curtain. Beside the booth there was a sign depicting two grumpy-looking figures in pantomime costumes, one of whom was wielding a truncheon. It read: 'Professor Jeffrey Lynne Presents Punch & Judy – Fun for All and All for Fun'.

'So what's a professor doing with puppets?' asked Clarissa.

'It's what they call a Punch and Judy performer. A Professor,' said George. 'It's a tradition.'

The puppets were jousting noisily now. Darting from one side of the claustrophobic stage to the other with their big stricken faces and stunted arms. One of them was now beating the other with a baton.

'Time for a taste of your own medicine, Mr Punch,' said Judy, wielding the baton in her big green dress and frilly bonnet. 'This is for not looking after my baby properly!'

There were cheers from the crowd.

'Hit him!' cried George, punching the air. He was suddenly possessed by an inexplicable urge to kill Mr Punch. 'Hit him hard! Pummel him!'

Several people turned around to look at George. He smiled meekly and pointed at the booth where Judy was still battering Punch. 'If something makes you itch, then scratch it,' she squeaked.

Suddenly a crocodile popped up between the two puppets, holding a plate of sausages. Judy hit the crocodile by mistake, and it reeled backwards. There was a dramatic pause as all three puppets froze and stared out at the crowd. Mr Punch then grabbed one of the sausages from the plate and started hitting Judy.

'What's all this, then?' said a puppet policeman appearing from the wings.

Mr Punch hit the policeman with the sausage. 'It wasn't me,' he yelled. 'The crocodile did it.'

George suddenly felt a hand on his shoulder.

'What's all this then?' said a stern voice.

George shuddered.

It was Perry, still in his shorts, with Bernard close behind. 'Thought we'd find you here,' he said.

'Oh, look,' said George, somewhat relieved. 'It's the blind man and the clown.'

'Well, I must be the clown, then,' said Bernard, seeing George and Clarissa arm in arm. 'Because I can see that you two are having fun.'

'We certainly are,' said George, gripping Clarissa's arm even more tightly than before.

'Well, it's time for the off, old boy,' said Perry.

'Good,' said Clarissa. 'It's turning bloody cold.'

'God, you're like a scratched record,' sighed George, as they turned to go.

They were still arm in arm, and for a second it looked as if she was smiling. 'Well, turn me over then,' she said.

George had a feeling that they would both remember this moment.

Drawing found in
Room 22, Bayview
Retirement Home

'Judy', dated June 1968

14

ONE FOR MY BABY

It was dawn, and George was sitting up in bed watching the light seeping from the edges of the dark-red velvet curtains. He'd been up half the night, since quarter to three, woken by the sound of cannon fire rolling around the sky. As well as the thunder there had been noises in his room, too. He'd called out for Tom, but he hadn't appeared. George's immediate instinct was to turn on the light, but as he reached over it felt as if someone's hand was trying to touch him. It didn't seem like a ghostly, otherworldly presence but a thumping physicality. He could almost feel the air being pushed apart by a fleshly frame as someone skulked among his things. So he lay there in the darkness, pretending to be asleep, feeling as if the walls were closing in on him. It was a long time before he plucked up the courage to move. Only when he could hear nothing but his own breathing did his hand creep out from under the covers towards the light switch.

The thunder had died away now as he sat there and stared at the curtains. It felt like the Blitz. He had been a toddler at the time and didn't know what he was hearing, but the distant explosions and the sound of the sky growling would stay with him for the rest of his life. He remembered seeing the fear on his mother's face. Not because they could be bombed at any moment but because his father was an air-raid warden.

The awful irony was that he died just after the war, when he was off duty. He'd become a fire warden, and he was out with a friend having a drink in the local pub. They'd only been in there for about ten minutes when an undiscovered bomb exploded on the premises. They were both injured, and George's father's wounds were fatal.

George remembered hearing the explosion and immediately knowing that something terrible had happened. It was as if the bomb had gone off in his head, not on the high street. Suddenly it felt as if the world was collapsing around him, but he didn't know why.

When the chief warden came to the house that evening to break the tragic news, he told them that their father had apparently tried to say something to the ambulance men before he died. They couldn't make out the words, but he thought they ought to know. His mother always insisted that he was telling them how much he loved his family.

He was given a hero's burial, of course, although little George couldn't actually look at the coffin. Instead, he stared up at the trees spread out across the sky like veins, while the brass band wheezed soft hymns on the grass and a bell tolled in the nearby church. His life would never be the same again.

There was more thunder now, like a sudden burst of violence from the next room. He remembered the puppets by the seaside with their big ripe faces, lunging at each other like truculent drunks in the wee small hours.

The room was getting lighter, at least. It looked like a sunny day behind the curtains.

Suddenly there was a knock at the door. He felt his stomach tighten.

'Are you awake in there, young man?' It was Serena.

'Give me a minute,' said George, slowly getting out of bed and opening the curtains. He opened the door, too.

'Ta-da!' she said. She was standing in the corridor holding a plate covered by what looked like a silver dome. 'Who's a lucky boy, then?' she said, proudly handing him the plate. 'I know it's a bit early, and I hope I didn't wake you, but I just thought you might like a special breakfast.'

'Thank you. But why?'

Serena smiled. 'It's for helping Clarissa yesterday . . . Are you coming down later? We've got our Hospitality Think Tank. We'd love to hear your views.'

'Er, yes, of course,' said George, looking at the plate. 'See you later. And thank you for my special breakfast.'

He closed the door behind her and secured the latch. He was feeling insecure, slowly starting to believe that he could trust no one. He sat down in the chair beside the window and removed the cover from the plate. The sun was shining outside. His special breakfast was sausages and fried bread, and for all he knew the sausages could be laced with strychnine. Which is why he began avidly devouring them one by one.

Having survived the sausages, George had decided to stick to the routine and go down to the Palm Lounge. Anywhere was better than sitting in his room. So far he'd made it to the hall where he was now studying the notice board at the bottom of the stairs.

HOSPITALITY THINK TANK: We always try our best, but nobody's perfect. So here's your chance to tell us what you think. Please join us in the Palm Lounge at 10 a.m. on Thursday to share your thoughts, good and bad, about our home.

He could hear Clarissa making her way along the corridor. She seemed to be talking to herself more than usual. 'Go on, put some money in the one-armed bandit,' he could hear her saying. 'You never know your luck.' She feigned surprise when she saw him. 'Shall we go in, then?' she said, gesturing towards the lounge. 'It's the Hospitality Think Wank. I think we've managed to miss most of it.'

They could hear Perry holding court as they approached the door. 'Well, Serena,' he was saying. 'I do have one minor complaint, about the loo roll in the toilet along the corridor out there. The perforations don't carry right across each sheet, which means a ragged tear.' There was a pause. 'So it's pot luck, so to speak, whether you get a scrap or a strip. Which makes the whole business rather tense. And rather long-winded, if you'll pardon the expression.'

Serena bit her lip. She was sitting upright in a chair with a clipboard, looking like she cared. 'Well, I can go and change the roll if you like.'

'Well, I'd give it a while . . .' said Perry, 'but it would be appreciated.'

'It's like those bloody lifts,' said Clarissa, marching into the lounge with George. 'I don't like going in them, not after someone else has been in there. Always needs a good airing.'

'Germs,' said June, who was sitting in the corner.

'I once went up to the top floor,' continued Clarissa, looking for a chair. 'My God, it was like Albert Steptoe hadn't wiped. Stank like bad teeth.'

'Well, I'm glad I didn't hear all this before I had my sausages,' said George, sitting down.

Serena stood up. 'OK, everyone,' she said, fondling her clipboard. 'Thanks for your input. And your output, Perry.'

'Hold on,' said Clarissa. 'You've haven't heard my complaints yet.'

'OK,' said Serena, sitting down again and trying to look interested. 'Please, go ahead, Clarrie.'

'Well, I haven't got any as it happens . . .' said Clarissa, finally lowering herself into a chair. 'But I might have done, and that's a complaint in itself. I mean, I hate the stairs, but then I hate stairs anyway . . .'

'Well, that's very helpful, Clarissa,' said Serena, standing up again. 'Thanks for your time, everyone. I shall endeavour to solve all of your complaints in due course. Perry, I'll check the toilet paper in about an hour or so . . . Also, just to let you know, the Palm Lounge is getting a makeover this week, so don't be surprised if you see decorators Harry and Johnny around the place. Karel – who some of you may remember from Upton Silver's performances – will also be helping out. They should be setting up later this afternoon.' She started handing out some leaflets. 'And, finally, I'd like to draw your attention to a couple of new classes some of you might be interested in. There. All done.'

Perry took a leaflet and saluted her with his good hand as she left the room, before changing the angle of the salute to make it look as if he was peering out to sea. 'My, my. Is that a drunken Dalek I see before me?'

Clarissa was ignoring him. She was too busy rummaging around in her bag, like a dog digging a hole. 'I know they're in here somewhere.'

'What are you looking for?' asked Bernard, who was sitting by the window with a notebook and pen.

'My glasses. I need them to read the bloody leaflet.'

'Frankly, I really wouldn't worry about it,' said Bernard, winking.

'That's easy for you to say, wanker.' She began barking obscenities into the bag. 'I mean, there's nothing in here...' At last she brought out a small brown leather case. 'Little fuckers,' she said as she opened it and put on the glasses.

'Careful you don't make a spectacle of yourself,' said Perry, briefly standing on tiptoe. Clarissa was still ignoring him.

'Now then, what the hell did I put these on for?' she said, still clutching the case. She shook her head. 'I mean, this is what happens, isn't it? You sit here in fear and just make yourself worse.' She took a hanky from her sleeve and wiped her nose. 'I'm getting pent up,' she said. 'I need one of those rabbit things.'

'I used to know a fellow who bred rabbits,' said Perry, trying to change the subject.

'I meant a vibrator,' said Clarissa.

Perry continued undaunted. 'Way back. Early fifties it was. Problem was, none of them ever came up to the exacting standards of the British Rabbit Council ... The Old English Spotit was one of the country's oldest breeds. That was the one to aim for apparently. Shame. He never felt he'd ... well, you know ... hit the mark.'

'It wasn't you, was it?'

George handed her the leaflet. 'Is this what you're looking for?' He could see a large name sticker on the case. 'So why does it say "Thomas" on your glasses case?' he asked. 'Are you sure they're yours?'

'Yes,' she said, staring up at him. The glasses made her eyes look huge. 'You think I'm mad, don't you?'

Bernard coughed.

'My son wears glasses,' she continued. 'He's called Thomas, and I want him to have this case when I die. I'm planning to put name stickers on everything in my room . . . Are you the glasses police or something?'

'Only asking,' said George.

She studied the leaflet. 'Look at this. There's a class where you sit there and remember your bloody childhood. It's called Memory Lane. But why would I want to remember a time when I was young and carefree and had my whole bloody life in front of me?'

'Attendance is not compulsory,' said Bernard.

'I mean, it's enough to make you jump out of the window. That's if I could get my buggering old body out of the bloody window. And if there were normal locks on the windows, not OAP-proof locks. Worse than child locks they are. Patronizing dickheads.'

'Well, why don't you try logging on at Byte Club instead?' said Perry.

'Are you talking in code or something?' asked Clarissa.

'No, it's that internet,' said Perry. 'Why not give it a go? The worldwide internet is apparently a wonderful thing. Invented by an Englishman, you know. A knight no less.'

'Oh, sod off. It's only been invented in the last couple of years. You'll be saying cars are Roman next.'

'No, I mean he's a sir,' said Perry.

'And you never know,' added Bernard. 'You might even end up on Facebook.'

'Oh, I don't know anything about that,' sneered Clarissa. 'I don't even know who it's by.'

'It's not a book,' said George. 'I think it's a webnet.'

'I know that, you dipshit. It's a webnet of a book . . . Or a book of a webnet with a face on it . . . Or something.'

'You can learn a lot from the intertel superhighway,' said

Bernard. 'Intestinal worms are actually meant to be good for you. I learnt that from a computer.'

'Don't get clever, dickhead,' said Clarissa.

'Well, somebody has to,' said Bernard, winking.

'Sorry, I didn't hear you,' said Clarissa. 'I was yawning.'

'They teach you how to use a mouse, too, apparently,' said Perry. 'And that's always useful.'

Clarissa shook her head. 'Honestly,' she sighed, 'if someone had told me thirty years ago that I'd be fondling a mouse in my old age, I'd have gone into a rage.'

'Well, I don't know,' said Bernard, shaking his head. 'You're a poet and you didn't know it, eh? I mean, what's the world coming to?'

'Try asking that little chap who used to live in the forest,' she said. 'He'd tell you.'

'What the hell are you talking about?' said Bernard. 'It sounds like one of Snow White's Dwarves.'

'No,' sniffed Clarissa. 'This one lived in Norway. And, anyway, you can't call them dwarves. It's offensive. They're handicapped midgets, like that Toulouse-Lautrec.' She got up from her chair and began squatting down in the middle of the room.

'What are you doing?' said Perry.

'I'm doing one of my exercises,' said Clarissa, putting her arms out in front her as she squatted. 'Saw it in a book. I'm proving I don't need a keep-fit class.'

'Well, I'm opening the window, just in case,' said Perry.

'So who's the Norwegian man, then?' asked Bernard.

'Hut in a forest, funny hair . . .' There was a pause. 'Aha!' she said at last, like Archimedes jumping from the bath. 'Wittgenstein.'

'So, has anyone else got anything fascinating to tell us all?'

asked George, noisily turning the pages of a broadsheet he'd taken from the reading-table.

'Well, I've got a nasal hair that's annoying me,' said Clarissa. 'It's like an insect's leg. I know I'll end up sticking nail scissors in my nose to get rid of it.'

Suddenly the fire alarm sounded.

'What's that shitting noise?' she snapped. 'Is it somebody's fucking mobile telephone?' She struggled to her feet and yelled. 'Turn it off! Turn it off!'

'Don't panic,' said Perry. 'Someone's probably just put a spoon in the microwave.'

'Now, please, everyone remain calm,' said Serena, hurrying into the room. 'I just need to check something . . .' She briefly left the lounge before returning in a slightly panicky state. 'OK,' she said. 'This is not a drill. I repeat, this is *not* a drill.'

'You're damn right,' said Clarissa. 'It's not a drill. It's one of those fucking mobile telephones. So why can't they turn it off?'

Serena swiftly began rounding everyone up. 'Quick as you can, please. All of you make your way out to reception. Come on, everyone. We need to make our way out to the courtyard at the front of the building.'

George belched loudly. The sausages were repeating.

One by one they all made their way into the hall, then to reception, before heading through the glass doors and out on to the forecourt. George was the last one out. He looked at all the residents as they stood there and remembered that first day he had gone down to the Palm Lounge. When they all gazed at him like zoo animals from their cages.

'Are you sure we're safe out here,' said Clarissa. 'I mean, I hope nothing's going to explode.'

'This isn't the war,' said Perry.

George felt like drowning him.

'But don't you think we'd be safer over there, near the road?' asked Clarissa.

'No, we're fine here,' said Serena. She raised her voice to address the residents. 'Now, everyone. Please stay put. I'm going to go back inside briefly to try to find out what on earth is going on.'

15

HEARTBREAK HOTEL

'I hate the spring,' said Clarissa, sitting on a low wall and staring at the plants. 'All that bloody *joie de vivre* gets right up my nose.'

Like everyone else on the forecourt she was waiting for Serena to reappear. She'd been gone for a while.

'Cheer up, Clarrie,' said George. 'For goodness' sake.'

'But why should I have any *joie*', said Clarissa, 'when I haven't got any bloody *vivre*? The springtime makes me feel old, and I hate being old. It creeps up on you like you're being hijacked by evil spirits. Eaten alive by the inability to stand up straight or walk more than a hundred yards without feeling half dead with your hands hanging down like a bloody chimpanzee.'

Perry appeared. He'd been wandering up and down the forecourt with his hands in his pockets. 'Morning, campers,' he said.

'And books,' continued Clarissa, undaunted. 'They get closer to your face with every passing year, while your face just gets heavier by the day, sagging like an old ceiling. There you are, growing a moustache, regardless of gender. Not knowing what day it is. Drinking Complan. Not hearing what people say. And when you do, not understanding it. And you're dry as a bone downstairs. Even if you weren't, who the hell would want to ride your old bones and your pocked-up cellulite flab anyway?'

'Frankly, my dear, I don't give a damn,' said Perry.

'I'm surprised you're not doing one of your crosswords, Perry,' said George, trying to keep the peace. 'Good for the soul, aren't they? Or something.'

'Good for the memory, old boy. Not the soul.'

'Well, why aren't you doing one then?'

'Can't remember where I put the damned paper, can I?'

Serena came back out on to the forecourt. 'Good news, everyone,' she said, trying to raise her voice above the general grumbling. 'Panic over. It was a false alarm after all.'

There was a collective grunt.

'I told you it was a bloody mobile phone,' said Clarissa.

'Well, one of the smoke alarms seems to have short-circuited,' said Serena, slightly embarrassed. 'Although it's a bit of a mystery as to how it happened. There was no reason for it just to go off like that. So, anyway, we can all go back inside now.' She gestured towards the entrance.

There was another collective grunt, this time followed by a tide of grumbling as everyone slowly made their way back into reception.

'I think there'll be a few complaints at the next Think Tank thingummy,' said Clarissa to Serena.

'Well, that's as may be,' said Serena, forcing a smile. 'But we didn't know it was a false alarm, and it's better to be safe than sorry.'

With everyone filing in like cattle, the crowded hall suddenly felt smaller and darker than before. Like a prison. Or, perhaps more accurately, a death camp. George was starting to feel claustrophobic, and it wasn't helped by having Clarissa at his side.

'I often have dreams about fire,' she said as they shuffled along. 'I once had one about trees bursting into flames. I was in a wood, too. Terrible it was.'

'Perhaps we can change the subject,' said George, pausing by the notice board and pretending to read it.

'I caught fire in that bloody wood. I was helpless.'

'Please,' snapped George. 'I don't want to hear about your dream.' There were looks from passing biddies. He took a deep breath and closed his eyes. The alarm had made the memory of his father's death all the more vivid. 'Perhaps I need my pills,' he said. 'I'm going to go back upstairs now and take my medication.'

'Don't go,' said Clarissa. There was panic written on her face. 'I'll be lonely without you.'

'Look,' he said, trying to calm himself down. 'I just don't want to hear any more about your stupid bloody dreams.'

'But I was only telling you because I don't think I want to use my Shoprider any more. I'm shit scared of bursting into flames. I always have been. I knew someone whose husband died in a fire in Cornwall. Cigarettes and suntan lotion – used to be flammable, apparently.'

'Well, it's your Shoprider,' said George, 'so it's up to you what you do with it.' He walked over to the lift and pressed the button to ascend.

Bernard suddenly appeared. 'What was that I heard, Clarrie?' he said. 'I didn't know you had an old flame in Cornwall. Can't keep any secrets around here, you know.'

'Sod off,' said Clarissa. 'I'm talking about someone who died in a fire.'

Bernard shook his head. 'I once knew a woman who had an electric blanket. Left it on all night. Woke up chargrilled.'

The lift arrived with a ping, and a very relieved George stepped inside.

'And you don't want any polystyrene tiles on the ceiling either,' said Bernard, peeking in and winking as the lift doors slowly closed. 'Or you'll go up like a torch.'

George closed his eyes as he ascended and imagined beating Bernard with a slapstick. Gradually he felt his anger subsiding as Bernard cowered under the blows.

Suddenly there was another ping. George opened his eyes and stepped out of the lift. The corridor felt colder than usual. He looked out of the window. The sky was grey. Thunder was lingering in the air.

As he stood there he thought about what Clarissa had said about growing old. He could remember that moment when he'd first felt as if life was slipping by. That moment when someone looks at you in a different way, as if you're no longer a player, just a spectator. And it came when he thought he was still young. Soon he'd start laughing at old people's jokes, knowing all the old faces and none of the new. Everything that used to be easy would suddenly become hard, while the hard would become nigh on impossible.

He could hear a voice now at the other end of the corridor. It sounded like an old man. 'Where are you?' the voice was saying. 'Come back to me ... please.'

The corridor was dimly lit, and George could see something moving in the gloom. It was small, but it was working its way steadily towards him along the floor.

He heard the voice again. 'It's time for lunch. I've got something nice for you. Please, come back to me ...'

George looked at the object as it approached. He could see a figure behind it now, which had slowly come into view as it turned the corner. It was an old man with a walking-stick, almost bent double with a stoop. He was wearing a striped shirt with baggy shorts and furry slippers.

'I need help,' said the old man as soon as he saw George. 'Elvis is escaping.'

George looked at the object inching its way towards him. He could see now that it was a tortoise. For a moment he watched the sluggish reptile outpace the old man, before kneeling down and blocking its way. Elvis stopped and turned his scaly head to one side. He looked up at George with a mournful eye.

'Sorry, old fella,' said George, picking him up and giving him back to the old man. 'But it's return to sender.'

The old man took the tortoise with a shaking hand and smiled. His glasses moved as his bulbous face momentarily changed shape. 'Thank you. I don't know what I'd have done if you hadn't been there. No one ever comes up here. They call it Lonely Street, you know.'

'What floor is it?' asked George.

'Top floor, of course,' said the old man. 'Was there some sort of alarm that went off a while ago?'

George nodded.

The old man shook his head and looked down at the floor. 'That'll be why Elvis was trying to escape.'

'Well, anyway, I'm glad I could be of help,' said George. He smiled and walked back towards the lift.

He could hear the usual thumps and bumps now as he stepped out on to the second floor and made his way towards his room. He'd wanted to return as soon as possible after the alarm, but the episode with the reclusive land-dwelling reptile – and the tortoise – had delayed him. However, as he stood at his door and fished around for the key the bumps gave way to shouts and the thumps gave way to screams. And they all seemed to be coming from Clarissa's room.

He went and stood outside her room and turned his ear towards the door. There were bangs, too, now, punctuated by yells and expletives. 'Get out of here,' she was shouting. 'Get out now.'

It was quiet for a moment, but then the door shook as another crash resounded.

'If you come any closer I'll scream,' he could hear her saying. 'Get out of here, you skeletal wanker!'

George knocked on the door. 'Clarissa, are you all right?'

There was another crash.

'No,' came the piteous reply. Her voice was muted, as if she was lying beneath something. 'Shit,' she yelled, 'I don't know what to do.' He could hear her crying to herself. 'I told you to go away,' she was saying. 'Now look what's happened. It's all your fucking fault . . .'

'Is there someone else in there with you?' asked George. There was no answer. 'Shall I get help?' He pushed the door, then backed away as it slowly opened.

'Oh God,' said George as he entered the room. 'Please don't let this be true . . .'

He could see a pool of dark red liquid on the floor, with a trail that led to the corner of the room. There was Clarissa slumped beside the chair, holding what looked like a small picture frame.

'Are you all right?' said George, almost tearful.

He was just about the pull the emergency cord when she replied. 'Of course I bloody am,' she said. 'I'm just having some grape juice after all the mayhem. Red's my favourite, and my hands were shaking. Spilt it all over the place.'

'But what happened after that?' asked George, sitting down in the nearest chair and looking at the chaos around him.

'The bookcase fell over. I was lucky it wasn't all hardbacks.'

George looked around the room. He could see the curtain flapping at the window like the wing of a huge bird.

'I've broken my son's picture,' she said, lifting herself up off the floor. 'It's the one I used to talk to every night. Such a bloody shame.'

'Don't worry. It's only the frame . . . So who was in here with you?'

Clarissa gave him a look. 'What are you implying?' she asked, looking as if she might hit him.

'I heard someone in here? Who was it?'

'Getting jealous, are we? Thought it was Bernard, did you? Puffing and panting away. Well, I used to be a cocktease, but now I'm just a decrepit old cow. There was no one here. It was just me and my old mum.' She pointed to a large patterned jar on a shelf with a small plaque attached to it. 'Thank God she's still intact.'

'So who were you telling to get out, then?' asked George.

'A fucking daddy longlegs, dickwit. It was driving me mad. That's what you get for trying to open the bloody window around here.'

'Well, perhaps we'd better close it, then,' said George, stepping over the books and making his way towards the window. As he looked out he could see Upton Silver's van parked outside, emblazoned with his spray-painted face. Available for parties, weddings and bar mitzvahs. And perhaps the occasional wake. 'I see Upton's back on the premises.'

'Yes. Karel is one of the decorators,' said Clarissa.

'Well, I hope nobody's performing.' He started clearing up the books.

'Here,' she said, handing him the keys to the Shoprider. 'You may as well have these while you're at it.'

'Are you sure?' said George, suddenly excited.

'Absolutely. But don't ride it along seaside promenades.'

George smiled. 'And what's this?' he asked, picking up what looked like a model fire engine.

'That's a model fire engine. The keys won't work on that. It's one of my son's old toys. Could have come in handy earlier.' She looked at the broken picture frame in her hand. 'I couldn't do the sound of a fire bell, so I used to say "Fire engine's coming" over and over again . . . Bit crap, I thought. He seemed to like it, though.' There were tears in her eyes now. 'He loved it when I blew a raspberry, too. And he liked the peep-o game, although that hurt my neck. Then there was the belching. I once nearly sicked up, though . . .' She took a hanky from her sleeve and blew her nose. 'You know, I can't remember life ever being much fun,' she closed her eyes and pressed her lips tightly together, 'but I'm sure it used to be better than this.' She began slowly shaking her head. 'It wasn't fair. Taking him away like that.' She looked at George. 'Taking them both away . . . We didn't have a chance. God's a shit, he really is.' She looked up at the ceiling and shook her fist. 'If you're up there, you fucking wanker, you're a shit! Do you hear me? You make me so lonely. If you come any closer I'll scream. You've taken everything away from me . . . Everything.' She started sobbing uncontrollably.

George was at a loss. Instinctively he put his arm around her, and she pressed her face to his chest like a baby.

'Why, George? Why?' she sobbed.

'I don't know, Clarrie.'

Gradually her crying subsided, and she pulled herself away

from him. She wiped her nose and sat for a while, sniffing. 'God's a cunt,' she sobbed. 'That's why.'

There was a knock at the door.

'Hello? Who is it?' said George.

'It's me,' said Serena. 'I've got a delivery for Clarissa. Can I come in?'

Clarissa nodded at George, and he opened the door. She seemed shocked as she came into the room. 'What's happened here?' she said, placing a brown parcel on the nearest surface.

'I had a little mishap,' said Clarissa. 'And Georgie was helping me to clear it all up.'

George left Clarissa's room, shutting the door firmly behind him. He'd never seen her like that before. He'd cleared up as much as he could, and she'd stopped crying at least. It was up to Serena now to do the rest.

He felt like barricading his own door with a chair as he went inside and turned on the light. It looked like rain again soon.

'Hello, pops,' said a voice near by. It was Tom. He was sitting in the corner of the room looking forlorn. 'I'm very sorry, really I am.'

'What for?' asked George. He always felt unduly troubled by Tom's apologies, the way he cowered slightly. 'Don't worry about it. Whatever you did doesn't matter.'

'But I thought it might help you,' said Tom. 'I know you want to get out of this place . . . It was me, you see . . . The fire alarm. I set it off.'

George couldn't help smiling. 'Was it really?' he said, with a tear in his eye. 'Good on you!'

Suddenly the light went out. Tom looked as shocked as George. There was a pause, followed by a yell from next door. George opened the door and looked outside in the corridor.

'What's happened to the bloody lights?' he could hear Perry asking.

Tom was now standing in the middle of the room.

'That's not me, pops,' he said. 'Promise.'

'Well, who the hell is it then?' said George.

Drawing found in Room 22,
Bayview Retirement Home

'Broken Woman', dated April 1964

16

FALLING IN LOVE AGAIN

'Hello. I'm here . . . Can you hear me now? . . . I said, I'm here
. . . Yes, at the home . . . Hello? . . . Yes . . . Can you hear me
now? . . . Hello? . . . Yes, the home . . . No, I'm here now . . . Yes
. . . the home . . . You're breaking up . . . I'll call you back . . . I
said I'll call you back . . . Bye . . . Yes, bye . . . OK, bye . . . Bye-
bye . . . Bah.'

George stood there in the hall, listening to the workmen in
the lounge. He'd tried the light switch again, but it was no use.

''Allo, bro,' said a voice in the gloom. It was Karel, carrying
a large toolbag through to the Palm Lounge.

'Hello.'

'Don't worry baaat da electrics,' said Karel as he passed.
'Johnny's putting some noo laaats out da back, so dey is off for
a few minutes.'

'Well, I wish someone had warned us,' said George.

'Ah don't fink dey knew,' said Karel. 'No worries. They'll be
back on pronto. Promise.'

'This place is going to pot,' said George as he followed Karel
into the lounge. 'It definitely needs a kick up the arse.' George
could see June stewing in the corner as usual, friendly as a
crocodile.

A bald and portly man wearing overalls was squinting at an

area just above the light switch. 'Afternoon, guv,' said the man. 'Sorry about the electrics. Normal service will be resumed as soon as we've sorted out these lights. Wanted to get them over with. Might rain later.' He belched. 'Oops. Pardon me,' he said, patting his stomach. 'Blame it on the boogie. I'm Harold, by the way.'

June glared at him from her corner with her painted face. 'As long as you haven't got a bloody dog,' she growled.

'Nice to meet you, Harold,' said George. He pointed at June. 'And don't mind her. She's always in a foul mood.'

Harold smiled. 'No probs, mate. We're used to eccentric characters.'

George sat down at the reading-table. It was the usual mind-numbing array of publications.

'Mind if I turn the radio on?' asked Harold, unscrewing a light switch.

'Not at all,' said George. He was bored rigid.

'I like a bit of music,' said Harold. 'Helps with the job. Some of those old classics, eh? Earth, Wind and Fire. Remember them?'

'Yes,' said George. 'Particularly the wind bit.'

Harold belched. 'Pardon me,' he said, patting his stomach. 'Can't hide love, eh?'

Nostalgic pop hits filled the room.

George had had enough of the reading-table and stood up. His intention was to move to the sofa. Instead he started moving to the music. Slowly at first, almost imperceptibly, starting with his legs and rising to his waist, culminating in a gentle but slightly painful swaying of the hips. He was now visibly rocking from side to side, moving his arms rhythmically in a kind of strange stirring action. Soon, though, he could feel his hips seizing up. What had once been sprightly steps had sadly become feeble footfalls.

'You could be on that programme,' said Harold, shifting a small table away from a plug socket. 'I bet you were a bit of a mover in your time.'

'This is still my time,' said George.

'No it isn't,' said June, giving him a stony stare.

Harold looked embarrassed. 'Sorry, guv. I meant I bet you were once a bit of a star on the dance floor.'

'I was indeed,' said George, suddenly stepping up the pace and attempting a spin, before colliding with the small table and falling headlong on to the floor.

'Christ, are you all right, mate?' said Harold, dropping his screwdriver and running to help.

'I think so,' said George, getting up, only to fall again as he slipped on one of the magazines.

'Shit. Shall I get someone?' said Harold. 'I'm really sorry about the table.'

'Oh, it can't be helped,' said George, lying on the floor. 'Really, I'm fine.' Then he grimaced and farted, shifting his left leg slightly to make the action a little more comfortable.

When he eventually did make it to the sofa the electricity came back on. He celebrated the resumption of power by turning on the television. Anything to block out the radio.

He could hear Clarissa now, talking to someone out in the hall. 'You won't find it down here, you daft bitch,' she was saying. 'I don't know why you're bothering. They'll all think you're a wanker for talking like this. But then they're all deaf, so it doesn't matter, does it?'

George wondered who she could be talking to, until finally she appeared in the doorway. Alone.

'I do hope these bloody builders don't make too much noise,' she said as she sat down next to him. 'Why are you watching this old black-and-white rubbish? Let's have something in colour, for God's sake.'

'It's called *The Punch and Judy Man*,' said George, dutifully reaching for the remote control. 'I thought you liked the seaside.'

'It's not good for you, all that grey,' she said. 'I'm depressed enough as it is. Weary all the bloody time. I put my polo neck on inside out just now. Had to talk myself out of a panic.'

'So what was in the parcel?' asked George.

She sighed and tried to force a smile. 'Something special for my little boy.'

George put his arm around her. 'I bet one of those channels is selling reversible jumpers,' he said.

'Oh, I can't be doing with all that,' said Clarissa, coming back to life. 'Not with that woman on there. Like the one in that soap opera with the little husband and the big nose.'

Bernard entered the room. 'Having fun, you two?' he said, winking and heading for the reading-table. He sat down and took a broadsheet from the pile. 'I apologize in advance for my lady friend.'

'Look at them clustering around me,' said Clarissa. 'They're like moths.'

'Oh hello, Bernard,' said George after a few moments. 'Sorry. I didn't see you there.' He could already feel his hackles rising.

'You know the woman I'm talking about,' continued Clarissa. 'That one who looks like an alien with her eyes wide apart. Thank God it's not one of those high-definition channels. I mean, that bloody *Eastdale Street* definitely needs to pull its socks up.'

'So what channel would you like, then?' asked George, confused.

'That one with the young man on it.'

'Well, that narrows it down,' said Bernard, fluttering his broadsheet.

'Foreigner,' said Clarissa. 'Funny name. Hair in tufts. Homosexual.'

Bernard sniffed theatrically and began fanning his face. 'Is there a funny smell in here? Or is it me?'

'Definitely you,' said George.

'He who smelt it dealt it,' said Clarissa.

'Oh, very original . . .' said Bernard. 'But it does smell in here.'

'Well, that'll make a change then,' said Serena, appearing from the kitchen.

'Germs,' said June from her corner.

'I think it's coming from that ivy thing over there,' said Bernard, pointing to a generic-looking plant in the corner and fanning his face even more furiously than before.

'Oi, bell end,' said Clarissa. 'Plants don't smell.'

'But it's dying. Look at it,' said Bernard.

'Does dying smell?' asked George. 'Why don't you ask your hair?'

'Dead things always smell terrible,' said Bernard, rattling his broadsheet. 'Remember Lenny? The whole corridor stank like a cowshed.'

'Well, I'll get the builders to take it away later, then,' said Serena, slightly irritable.

'Don't get me started,' said George, leaning forward on the sofa. 'Oops, stand clear,' he said, farting loudly. 'Sorry, I had sausages for breakfast. Can't be helped.'

For a moment there was silence. Even Serena seemed a little shocked.

'Oh, for pity's sake,' exclaimed Bernard suddenly, using his broadsheet as a giant fan.

'Christ, Georgie,' said Clarissa, waving her hand in front of her face. She paused. 'Actually, it's not all that bad. Reminds me of broccoli soup. And, anyway, I can't talk. I was terrible this morning. You know when you think you haven't done anything except a smell. Then you look down, and it's like a bucket of eels.'

'Serena,' said Bernard, 'can you find out if one of the workmen urinated in it please?'

George could feel himself getting angry.

'No I can't,' said Serena. 'Why would they? I think they've got their own portable toilet in the garden. Would anyone like any tea?' she said, disappearing into the kitchen.

'Is it that thing that looks like it's from *Dr Who*?' said Clarissa.

'Yes,' said George. 'They call it the Turdis.'

Perry appeared in the doorway. 'Hi-de-hi, campers,' he said as he made his way to his usual chair. 'Been spreading some of your holy water around again, have you, George?'

'Can't you knock?' said Clarissa. 'Georgie boy has just made a bloody awful smell.'

Perry nodded sagely, then cracked his knuckles. 'I know. I heard it in reception.' He pointed to a man grimacing on the television. 'And he doesn't look too pleased about it either.'

'Oh, that's just the actor's lot,' sighed Bernard, having switched broadsheets. 'Inner turmoil and all that.'

'I bet you know how that feels, eh, Bernie?' said Perry.

'Not at all,' sniffed Bernard. 'It was entirely my choice to stop appearing alongside the likes of Harry Worth.'

'Oh God,' huffed Clarissa. 'I think I prefer your farts, George.' She scowled at Bernard. 'Why don't you go out and see to your vegetables? Make sure the builders aren't pissing all over them.'

'Oh yes, the veggies,' said Perry, trying to change the subject. 'How are they coming along?'

'Oh, we're fine.'

Bernard ignored her. 'Splendidly. Thank you, Perry.'

'So where exactly do you grow them?' asked George, suddenly interested.

'Out the back there, in the corner. All they need is a little TLC and some manure.'

'Well, I can help you there,' said Clarissa.

'Do you have a favourite vegetable, George?' asked Bernard haughtily.

George thought for a moment. 'I tried fennel once, but it tasted of urinals.'

'Er, not actually a vegetable . . .' smirked Bernard.

'I was referring to Florence fennel,' said George. 'Which is definitely a vegetable.'

'If you say so.'

'Well, I don't say so, it just is.'

'I'm more of a courgette-and-tomato man myself,' sniffed Bernard. 'I tried growing sweet peas once, but the pigeons ate them. It's all organic, of course.'

'Oh, shut up,' said Clarissa. 'Everything's bloody organic. It means nothing. I grew organic vegetables when I was first married. Lived next door to a right stuck-up old cow. Her husband wasn't much better. We had chickens, too, and a goat. We even generated our own electricity.'

'No you didn't,' said George. 'That was *The Good Life*. It was a comedy series on the television.'

She looked bewildered for a moment. 'Was it? So I suppose me being a detective in a village and solving local crimes, that's all made up, too, then, is it?'

'Yes,' said George.

'Don't panic,' said Perry.

'Still, at least I'm not a guillemot,' sighed Clarissa. 'I heard a programme about them on the radio. The polar bears are eating them all in Canada.'

'Would anyone like any tea?' asked Serena, bringing in a tray and placing it on the table.

'Don't mind if I do,' said Clarissa, getting up.

'I've already made some for our workmen friends,' said Serena. 'Please bear with them as they move about the lounge.'

'Saw one of them just now,' said Clarissa. 'Looked like a loon. Walking up and down outside, chatting away to himself with a big hearing aid, saying "Can you hear me now? I'm breaking up." And he was wearing a necklace.' Serena poured Clarissa a cup of tea. 'End up beige again, will it?' said Clarissa, taking her tea back to the sofa.

'Well, it'll look like beige,' said Serena. 'But the colour's actually called A Touch of Fossil.'

George thought for a few moments. 'Otherwise known as Foul Host Fiasco.'

Serena looked baffled. 'Yes, thank you. And the window frames will be Victorian Vanilla.'

'A Convivial Art Nil,' said George. 'It's an anagram.'

'What's an anagram?' asked Clarissa.

'It's when you rearrange the –'

'I know what an anagram is. I meant, *what's* it an anagram *of*?' said Clarissa, sitting down then quickly standing up again. 'Oh, for Christ's sake,' she said, wiping her polo neck with her free hand. 'I'm bloody spilling everything nowadays. I don't want to. I just can't help it. And I've lost my glasses.' She was starting to panic. 'What am I going to do?' She sat down, looked down at her lap and closed her eyes. George put his arm around her again. 'All that's left now is the bloody rocking chair,' she said.

'Are you all right?' asked Serena, squatting down beside her.

Clarissa nodded. 'Let me go upstairs,' she said. 'They're calling me. I need to change my clothes.' There were tears in her eyes now. 'And I think I've just pissed myself.'

Serena helped Clarissa up and took her out of the lounge. George turned off the television. For a while nobody spoke. Not even Perry. It was one of the workmen who finally broke the silence.

'Do you mind if I measure up for the curtains?' said the man, entering the lounge from the garden. He was thin with an almost constant smile. 'Won't take a minute,' he said. 'Fitting some new ones tomorrow. My name's Jack, by the way.'

'Please go ahead, Jack,' said George. 'I wouldn't hamper the hangman.'

The man suddenly looked a little uneasy. 'I'm going to have to close them for a moment, if nobody minds,' he said, pulling the curtains noisily along the rail before setting up a stepladder in the corner right next to June. Bernard sighed loudly at the reading-table as darkness enveloped the room.

George felt uncomfortable in the dark. He could see June's painted face staring up at the man as he stepped up on to the ladder and began measuring the hem. He was now only inches away from her. 'You better not have a dog,' she said.

The workman looked down for a moment. He appeared shocked. After a few moments he stepped down and moved the ladder to the other side of the room, measuring as he went. 'Thank you,' he said at last, opening the curtains again. 'Sorry for any inconvenience.' He went back out into the garden.

George had decided to go upstairs. He felt tired and defeated, unsure of what his next step should be. It was still stormy outside, and the corridor felt narrower than usual. Airless and cloying, like the passage through a train carriage. He was concerned about Clarissa. She'd plummeted again when she spilt her tea.

As he made his way reluctantly along the corridor he could hear noises. Not the usual thumps and bumps and muffled yells. This was more like the sound of a siren, followed by a voice chanting some words over and over like a mantra.

George was outside Clarissa's door now. It was ajar. He could finally hear what the voice was saying. 'We're on our way, on our way. On our way to save the day.'

The voice sounded robotic, agreeable at first but soon becoming soulless and eventually downright menacing. A vacuous voice vaguely fitting the mechanical notes beneath it. And it was playing over and over again.

'We're on our way, on our way. On our way to save the day.'

There was a pause at the end of each line. A moment filled with hope that it would finally stop. But no . . .

'We're on our way, on our way. On our way to save the day.'

George was beginning to feel as if he was being brainwashed. He thought about the old mobile that used to hang above his cot when he was a baby. Little cut-out figures hanging in the air, going around and around to the sound of a musical box plinking out a lullaby.

'We're on our way, on our way. On our way to save the day.'

He knocked on the door. It opened a little more. 'Clarissa?'

'We're on our way, on our way. On our way to save the day.'

'Clarissa, are you in there? It's me,' he said. 'Isn't that noise driving you mad?'

'We're on our way, on our way. On our way to save the day.'

He knocked again. He could feel his heart thudding. He was beginning to struggle for breath.

'We're on our way, on our way. On our way to save the day.'

'Clarissa,' he yelled. The volume of his voice caught him by surprise, and, as an absurd and instinctive attempt to counterbalance, he whispered her name to himself.

'We're on our way, on our way. On our way to save the day.'

There were tears in his eyes as he slowly pushed the door open.

He could see the silhouette of a small figure standing by the window. It looked like a young boy. He was crying and pressing his little fists to his eyes as he stared down at Clarissa, who was lying on the floor in front of him. She'd opened the brown parcel and seemed to be clutching some kind of toy. 'We're on our way, on our way. On our way to save the day.'

The room was unusually cold, and George was beginning to feel uneasy. 'Tom?' he said. His voice was faltering. 'Is that you?'

The boy ran behind the curtain, covering his face with his hands.

'Clarissa, are you all right?' said George, as he walked slowly towards her.

He knelt down beside her. He could see contusions on her face, a swollen bruise on her cheek. Her hand was resting on the toy. It was a fire engine. Her fingers were placed on the button that was playing the recorded message. As he lifted her hand the room was suddenly engulfed in throbbing silence, kept afloat by the tick-tock of the battery-powered clock on the shelf near by.

He looked around. The little boy had gone, and he could hear voices outside in the corridor.

'Wait! Stand aside,' said Serena, rushing into the room. There was panic on her face as she put her finger on Clarissa's neck. After a few moments she shook her head and looked at George.

'She's gone,' she said, with tears running down her cheeks. 'And may God go with her.'

17

WHAT A DIFFERENCE
A DAY MAKES

George had gone back to his room. He couldn't face seeing anybody. For a while he sat by his window, staring at the outside world through the grey net curtains as the toy fire engine repeated its mantra over and over in his head.

'We're on our way, on our way. On our way to save the day . . .'

There were voices in the corridor now as people went in and out of Clarissa's room. He was dreading a knock at the door and an invitation to the Palm Lounge. Maybe they would think that he was dead, too, if he didn't answer. Perhaps he was. It was hard to tell.

Serena did eventually knock on his door, but it was to enquire about dinner. He said he wasn't hungry, and for once she took him at his word. So he sat there in his chair with his stomach rumbling and drifted off to sleep.

He woke up in the early hours. The room was in darkness, and the only light was from the streetlamp on the forecourt seeping in from behind the curtains. He'd been woken by a noise. Not a sudden noise but a gentle series of sounds that had somehow reached a crescendo and woken him from his slumber. He could sense that there was someone in the room now. He couldn't see anything, but someone was definitely there.

'Tom?' he whispered. 'Is that you?'

He heard a noise near by. It sounded like someone brushing up against the curtain or perhaps a breath or even a foot on the carpet . . . Someone or something was definitely in the room.

As he stood up and opened the curtains to let in the light from the streetlamp he spied a small figure hiding beside the bed. Suddenly it jumped out into the room.

It was Tom. 'Morning, pops,' he said, smiling. He seemed excited.

'It's still early, isn't it?'

'But I've got someone with me,' said Tom, pointing to the armchair George had been sitting in.

'The chair's empty.'

'I know,' smiled Tom. 'She's over there, behind it.'

Suddenly a figure jumped out from behind the chair.

George felt his heart leap.

It was Clarissa, smartly dressed as if for a special occasion. And she looked happy. Happier, in fact, than he'd ever remembered seeing her.

'Fancy a fandango?' she asked.

He was stunned. He couldn't speak. She looked younger and fitter, and she was actually smiling.

'Come on. Turn the radio on, Georgie,' she said.

Nervously George walked over to the radio and pressed the on button. An upbeat pop hit from the past began pulsing from the speaker, albeit at low volume. Clarissa looked at Tom. He smiled, and they both began moving to the music. Tom was copying Clarissa as she smooched from side to side. George closed his eyes for a moment, then opened them again. They were still there, smiling and laughing as they jived and jitter-bugged, bopped and bodypopped, all in the glow of the streetlamp from the forecourt.

'Why don't you join us?' said Clarissa. 'We're having fun . . . Remember fun, Georgie?'

Fun was a distant memory for George, it was true. But he wasn't going to chance it again after his antics in the Palm Lounge. In fact, even watching them was making his left knee throb, so he squatted down and stared at the floor to ease the pain.

'Looks like it's time to have some fun with the scooter, eh, George?' he heard her say while she was waltzing to a guitar solo. 'You've got the key now. And it's so much better than a stick.'

George smiled to himself and looked up at Clarissa, but she wasn't there. Tom had gone, too. The room was empty now, so he turned off the radio and crawled into his bed.

'What shall I do with the scooter?' he asked, as he lay there in the glow of the streetlamp.

'You said I was like a scratched record when we were on the beach,' said a voice near the bed. He couldn't see her, but he knew it was Clarissa. 'So all you need to do is start from scratch.'

'Good morning, George. How are you feeling today?'

The loud but lacklustre female voice bellowing on the Tannoy caught him every time.

He yawned, stretched and rubbed his eyes, then pressed the small red button beside his bed.

'I'm feeling fine,' he replied.

'That's good to hear,' said the voice. 'Now you have a great day, won't you?'

There was a click. George breathed a sigh of relief. He would indeed have a great day. He would make sure of it. His new mission was to have fun. And it would all start with the scooter.

He was feeling strangely inspired by the events of the early hours as he donned his crimson flared trousers, pale-green shirt and red-striped trainers for the third day running. They were starting to smell, but it didn't matter. They'd seen a lot of action in the past few days, and they were about to see some more. He could already hear the builders downstairs as he carefully folded the striped silken cap, put it in his pocket and left the room.

Portly Harold was kneeling on a dustsheet in the Palm Lounge, opening a large tin of paint with a screwdriver. 'Mornin', guv,' he said.

'And what a lovely morning it is,' said George. 'Bit of a change from yesterday.' He looked around at the room. There was June in the corner, as usual. 'You really are doing a great job.'

'Er, we haven't done that bit yet.'

'Of course . . . I knew that. I meant generally.'

There was a pause. Harold stood up and belched. 'Oops, pardon me,' he said, patting his stomach.

George cleared his throat. 'Can I ask you a favour?' he said. 'Do you have a small screwdriver and a Stanley knife I could borrow for a couple of hours?'

'I certainly do,' said Harold. He lowered his voice. 'But don't tell Serena I lent them to you. You know what she's like.'

George nodded, then tapped his nose in a conspiratorial gesture.

Harold rummaged around in his tool bag. 'Slot or Pozidriv?'

George wanted to say 'The sharpest you've got' but resisted the temptation. 'Slot's fine.'

Harold handed him the tools. George thanked him and left the lounge.

He could hear Harold belching as he made his way back upstairs. 'Pardon me,' he heard him say. 'Return to sender.'

The sky was blue as George made his way out to the car park. He could see the Shoprider parked in its usual place. His knee was definitely feeling better now, although he didn't want to overdo it. He'd spent the last hour trying to fit the screwdriver to his red-striped Nike trainer, nearly stabbing himself in the process, making a hole in the side so that it poked out like a spike. What he'd really wanted was a bayonet and a sledgehammer, but he'd thought better of it.

Taking a deep breath, George donned his silken cap and climbed aboard the scooter. He could feel Clarissa close by as he turned the key in the ignition and watched the dials come alive, telling him it was fully charged. He took a deep breath and pressed the accelerator. The scooter moved silently across the Tarmac. He paused before crossing the forecourt, took another deep breath, then sashayed up the path like an automaton poised to terrorize the streets. The red roses by the church on the corner looked like sores on the old grey walls as he sped by. He was now travelling at full throttle, the same speed as a jogger with gout.

There were no surprises when he reached the high street. It was late morning and thus full of grumpy mothers with pushchairs assuming right of way. He glided past Edmunds Cut Price Store (apostrophe-free). He was already having fun driving headlong at the phone zombies before suddenly sounding his shrill horn. The shock on their faces was palpable.

It made George feel warm inside. Today, though, he'd be starting from scratch. So it was the side-roads he was aiming for.

He crossed the high street, pausing at a traffic island and shuddering as the cars sloped by on either side. At last he turned the corner and surveyed the road ahead. It was ripe and ready for his lethal spur. The trees were lush and green, and there was a fine display of cars, with their bodywork snug against the kerb. He would target bloated four-wheel drives and overdressed saloons. If he was lucky there might even be one or two sporty models; low-slung gas guzzlers that think they're racing cars. He couldn't wait to see the paint flake off like dead skin as the screwdriver screeched its way along the doors.

He remembered combing the streets when he was a boy looking for German cars so that he could scratch them with his penknife, in the hope that it would bring back his father. It never did, of course, but it made him feel a whole lot better.

The war was over by then. But that's like telling someone in a wheelchair to stop fretting because the person that ran them over has now been fined. For years afterwards he'd watch his mother waiting for the wailing sirens as the daylight faded and the lights went on in all the houses. There she'd be, another puppet at the window, another weary face above the flaking sills, with the trees hissing and shifting against the ever-darkening backdrop. A dim phantom through the dirty glass, forever bent towards a task, with the weight of the world on her shoulders.

George slowly made his way along the pavement on what was now his very own Go-Get ES5 Ultra Light mobility scooter. Having checked the street for passers-by and faces at the windows, he was ready to go to war. With his foot pressed hard into his shoe, thus securing the screwdriver, he ventured carefully towards the kerb, swaying back on to the pavement as the trees dictated.

His first casualty was a shiny blue saloon. It was more of a scratch than a wound but a disfigurement none the less. From here on he would be merciless, with the Stanley knife stepping in whenever it was needed. He did himself proud with a jumped-up silver wagon, jabbing the four-wheel-drive tyres like they were spuds waiting to be baked. His only regret was that he couldn't get to the spare.

Suddenly the euphoria ended.

Parp-parp-parp. He'd set off an alarm.

It was a German station-wagon, and within seconds of the screwdriver touching the bodywork it was flashing its lights and hooting hysterically like a toddler having a tantrum. Three ghastly parping notes repeated over and over.

It was now all systems go, for what it was worth. He could hear the alarm behind him. He pulled the cap from his head and crammed it in his pocket. Parp-parp-parp. He didn't want to look in the wing mirror in case he crashed into a lamp-post. Parp-parp-parp. So he just kept on going, with the paving stones beating a tattoo beneath him. Parp-parp-parp. Full throttle. Parp-parp-parp. Heart pounding. Parp-parp-parp.

At last he turned the corner on to the high street. For a moment he was Ernie, the fastest milkman in the west, swerving as he headed back towards Bayview. The car alarm sounded faint now as he crossed the forecourt and parked the Shoprider in its usual spot, then dismounted as quickly as he could.

He'd heard something banging in the Velcro bag at the back as he'd juddered along, so he fished through the keys and undid the little padlock. It was a wheel lock that had been banging. But with it was a package. A padded yellow envelope, unsealed. George took out the package and snapped the padlock closed again. He wanted to distance himself from the Shoprider as soon as possible.

On his way back to the forecourt he passed the dustbins. He stopped. There, beside the huge metal bins, was the sofa that used to be in the Palm Lounge. He couldn't believe they were throwing it out. He'd been sitting on it only yesterday with Clarissa at his side.

He sat down on the sofa and looked at the package in his hand. It felt heavy. He opened it and pulled out Clarissa's battered white envelope of coins. He could see some writing on the back that read 'First takings 1966'. He also found her bus pass and two old photographs. One of them was a wedding photograph. An old Polaroid of Clarissa with her skirt billowing and her husband close beside her. He thought of Judy and remembered waking in the darkness with the stars splashed across the black sky. Two lovers let loose on each other, warming the old stone of the house with their passion. He looked at the other picture. It was of Clarissa again. She was smiling, pointing to a little boy on her knee wearing a blue jumper.

He could sense someone beside him now. He said goodbye to the sofa and stood up. There were tears in his eyes as he made his way towards the glass doors.

There were two large dogs sitting by the entrance, bull terriers both. One of them started fretting as George passed by. Standing and sitting and standing again, licking the glass and leaving saliva smears like snail trails. The other one started growling. They looked abandoned, despite the fact that they had collars and were tethered to the bicycle rack.

The Palm Lounge was abandoned, too, except for June who was stewing in the corner as usual. He'd come to return Harold's screwdriver and Stanley knife, but there was a tray of empty cups and leftover biscuits on the table, so they were obviously on a break.

George glanced over at June. It took courage. She was getting more menacing by the day. She stared back at him with stony eyes, her bleak face with its thin red lips and ovoid chin framed by her headscarf.

'Good riddance,' she said.

George was baffled.

'Clarissa,' barked June. 'Good riddance to her.'

George suddenly felt a wave of anger rising inside him. 'If something makes you itch, then scratch it,' he could hear Judy saying.

He went over to the table, grabbed the plate of biscuits and marched out to reception. Checking that the coast was clear, he went out to the forecourt and untied the dogs. Tempting them inside with biscuits and teasing them until they were at breaking point, he lured them into the lounge with their leads trailing behind them.

June screamed when she saw them.

'Biscuits on the menu,' said George, as he emptied the plate over her and let the dogs do their work. 'You dogs were Heaven sent.'

June was beside herself, retching and coughing as the dogs sprang at her, with George egging them on. She started yelling for help, screaming and grasping at life like a poltergeist. She tried to get up but was pushed back by one of the dogs that was now growling at her while the other dog was busy rutting her leg, thrusting back and forth as if his life depended on it.

She started coughing hysterically, hawking like a vulture, choking. Suddenly she closed her eyes, moved her head back as if in slow motion and let out a God-almighty sneeze. Her head shot forward, together with her teeth, which flew out on to the carpet.

The dogs seemed shocked, instinctively backing away. George grabbed their leads and quickly led them back outside. He could hear June banging on the window.

'When are they coming?' she yelled. 'When are they coming?'

Suddenly the window shattered.

George could hear her shouting for help as he went back upstairs to his room.

He had to get away from Bayview. And there was no time like the present.

Drawing found in Room 22,
Bayview Retirement Home

Untitled (written on the back: 'When are they coming?'),
dated June 1980

18

OVER THE RAINBOW

There was a knock at the door. It seemed louder than usual, more emphatic. For a moment George considered hiding under the bed. Perhaps it was the police. He walked carefully over to the door and put his ear to the cold veneer. There was another knock. He felt it this time, as well as being nearly deafened by it, and it sent him reeling back into the room.

'I know you're in there,' said a voice from the corridor. It sounded like Serena, but he couldn't be sure.

'Don't come in,' said George, his ears still ringing. 'I'm not decent.'

He quickly took the striped silken hat from his pocket and shoved it in the wooden box under his bed.

'I need to talk to you,' said the voice. It sounded stern.

George was feeling anxious now. He briefly looked towards the window and considered climbing out. But nobody ever does that in real life, so he took a deep breath, plucked up courage and opened the door.

It was Serena. She was holding a package and looking serious. It was another padded yellow envelope.

'I need to talk to you,' she said, without the usual warm smile.

George nodded like a guilty schoolboy and ushered her in.

'It's about the Shoprider,' said Serena, making her way towards the chair by the window. 'Did you use it this morning?'

'Well, yes,' replied George, now perched on the bed. There was no way he could lie.

Serena sat down. 'And did Clarissa give you the keys before she . . . went to a better place?'

'Of course,' said George. It felt like he was being cross-examined by the police.

She sighed. 'So where did you take the Shoprider this morning, then?'

'Er . . . the high street mainly,' stammered George. 'I just wanted to try it out . . . to see how it went.' He could feel his stomach acid rising above his lower oesophageal sphincter and up into his gullet. He felt like vomiting.

'Well, I have some bad news. Unfortunately I've been informed that Clarissa left no written proof that she was passing the Shoprider on to you, so I'm afraid I must ask you for the keys.'

There was a pause. George's stomach acid was slowly returning to sender.

'Well,' he said, 'that is bad news . . . So is that what you wanted to talk to me about?'

'Not quite,' said Serena, holding up the package. 'I also have another splendid yellow envelope for you. I'll swap you for the keys.'

George nodded and did the business, relieved that he'd rescued the coins from the back of the Shoprider. He then showed Serena to the door.

'I'm sorry,' she said, hoisting a brief smile as she stepped out into the corridor, 'but they're sticklers around here. They have to be.'

George shrugged and shook his head, then closed the door behind her.

After a few moments he wandered over to the window and looked out at the trees. They were lush and green, made all the more garish by the grey cloud that was filling up the sky. They weren't as vivid as a rainbow, but they did the job. He stood there admiring the view, stock-still and caught up in his thoughts. It wasn't the world that he disliked. It was the people in it.

He could hear voices on the forecourt now. He feared it was the police, but he didn't dare look down to check. Perhaps he'd been a little rash vandalizing the cars. One thing was clear, though, it was definitely time to leave Bayview. It couldn't be any clearer if they'd sung it over the Tannoy.

A couple of hours later George was ready to go. He'd packed his bag and was now standing by his chair, looking around the room for the last time. Beneath his grey coat he was still wearing his crimson flares and pale-green shirt, but he'd swapped his punctured red-striped trainers for a pair of featureless brown loafers. He would take the trainers with him and dispose of them as soon as possible.

He looked at the yellow envelope unopened on the sideboard behind the framed photos. It could stay there and rot with the rest of the Bayview residents for all he cared. The word 'Condolences' written on the back was more than enough to put him off opening it. He was finally ready to go back home and restart his life.

He was starting to feel genuinely excited, and as he walked to the door he could feel a little jig coming on. In fact, he felt a little lightheaded. Suddenly he felt short of breath. He sat down on the bed with his heart pounding. He was gulping for air now. Grabbing loud and laboured breaths between deathly pauses. After a few minutes the panic subsided, and he sat there, his chest still heaving, trying to gather his thoughts.

He'd already thrown out the piles of unopened foil-wrapped pills that he'd been hoarding since his arrival at Bayview, so he couldn't even resort to trumped-up tranquillizers. Instead, he remembered Judy's words and thought of something he loved. And this time it worked. 'Be it ever so humble,' he whispered, 'there's no place like home . . .'

It was definitely time to go.

He walked to the door, took a deep breath and stepped out into the hall for the very last time. As he turned the key in the lock he heard a pinging sound near by. It was Horace coming out of the lift.

'Yoo-hoo,' he said as he marched up the corridor towards George. 'Don't I know you?'

He was wearing the same blue suit as before, with the trousers slightly paler than the jacket. It was the colour of a cold spring sky. His shoes, meanwhile, were brown and chunky like Cornish pasties, and his socks were thick, unlike his trousers, which were made of fabric so unnaturally thin that it would almost certainly be classed as a membrane in the natural world. 'You didn't bring me anything back from your trip.'

'I'm so sorry,' said George, 'but that's why I'm off again now.' He pointed at the bag.

'I'm Horace, by the way,' said the man, offering George his hand. 'Also known as Professor Felkin.'

George nodded and shook his hand.

'I'd offer you a cracker,' said Horace/Professor Felkin, fishing around in his pocket and bringing out a grubby brown serviette, 'but I seem to have run out of them.'

'Well, thank you for the thought,' said George, trying to

push past, 'but I must dash. It was nice to see you again.'

'Wait a minute,' said Horace/Professor Felkin, blocking his way. 'I have something for you.' He fished around in another pocket and brought out a brown envelope. 'Would you be kind enough to post this letter for me? It's a blueprint for one of my inventions.'

'Certainly,' said George, putting the envelope in his bag.

'I've invented a walking-stick that becomes a ladder in case you're attacked by a dog,' said Horace/Professor Felkin. 'It was that or the machine for nullifying radio signals from hidden implants.' He leant towards George. 'This arm,' he whispered, 'it isn't actually mine, you know.'

George nodded, in sympathy as much as anything else, before saying his goodbyes and making his way downstairs. He had two more tasks to perform before leaving Bayview.

The Palm Lounge was still deserted. June's corner was empty, and the window that she'd broken had already been replaced. The curtains had been taken down, and there were now sheets laid out on the floor in front of the skirting-boards. George carefully placed the screwdriver and Stanley knife beside a pot of paint where portly Harold would see them. That was task number one.

Next he tried the door into the garden. He was looking for the corner where Bernard grew his vegetables. It was easily spotted. There was a small placard in front of it, bearing the legend 'Bernie's Patch'. On it there was a poem:

> This corner of a foreign field
> Does offer up its veggie yield.
> Organic, yes, and only so,
> For those above the normal Joe.

George sighed, then put his bag down and unzipped his flies. This was task number two, to put the organ back into organic, as he urinated all over the courgettes. He couldn't conjure up any manure, but he was more than making up for it with an impressive arc of golden bodily fluid. The tomatoes were next, as the urinary equivalent of heavy rain battered the bushy leaves.

At last he was finished. His bladder was totally empty. So he zipped up his flies, picked up his bag and went back into the Palm Lounge. He took a last look. It was the end of an era. The lounge would never look the same again, blessed as it would now be with a mix of Victorian Vanilla and A Touch of Fossil. He said his goodbyes and made his way out to reception.

As he walked out on to the forecourt he could see Horace/Professor Felkin waving from the window. George took the brown envelope from his bag and held it up for him to see. Horace/Professor Felkin gave him the thumbs-up and mouthed the words 'Koran dankon', Esperanto for effusive thanks. George was on his way at last, and Bayview would soon be alive with it. The excitement might even prolong the lives of some of the fossils who lived out their grey lives there, separated by the thin plasterboard walls. He'd have been dancing up the path towards the high street if it hadn't been for the sudden pangs of arthritis. He passed the church on the corner. The roses still looked like sores, but at least he'd finally be rid of them.

He was standing at the bus stop now, outside Edmunds Cut Price Store (no apostrophe), studying the route map. He'd tried sitting on one of the plastic bench seats in the bus shelter, but it had been impossible. So he stood there and admired the view, watching the middle-aged cannonball bellies lurching past Edmunds (no apostrophe) desperate bargain offers, and the hooded youths with their rolling gaits like thin men with a fat man's walk. He was relieved when the bus finally arrived.

George had taken Clarissa's travel pass from her bag without realizing that it had her photograph on it. He'd have to think quickly. As the bus drew up and opened its doors, he flashed the pass in front of the driver, carefully obscuring the photograph with his fingers and diverting his attention by pretending he was in pain. It worked. Soon he was making his way upstairs to the almost-empty top deck, where he found a window seat and settled down.

As the bus moved off he looked down at the street as it slipped away beneath him. The glass was smeared and stained with rain, but he could still see the park with its lush flowerbeds like garlands on mass graves. He watched the joggers gurn as they ruined their hips, while the children with their sparrows' bones played in the playground and the swifts screamed overhead.

George had always loved swifts. He remembered the time when he was a boy, how one of them had landed on a window-sill above him. It was as if it had crash-landed from another world. The windowsill had been spiked to keep birds off, and he could see the panic in its eyes. They were wide with it. The bird was skewered, wildly looking this way and that as the pain engulfed it. Exhausted from its ceaseless flight, it was bleeding and flapping its wings. George had wanted to reach up and help it, but there was nothing he could do. And when he tried, the swift's panic only grew. He'd often felt like he'd crash-landed on this dreadful earth, too. Doomed to roam its grey streets like a man in purgatory, until a way back finally presented itself.

He looked out at the chimney tops along the weary streets. Little plots of land made sacred, filled with tiny King Lears in sweaty tea-stained rooms, buried in their sagging sofas with their televisions and quick fixes, sating their senses until it all seemed vaguely tolerable. Perhaps this was peace, thought George, to live your life out on the sidelines, content to watch the daylight drain away and the colours changing in the room as the roots of defeat slowly thicken beneath the floorboards. Never rocking the boat or making a scene, just squatting beneath the sagging slates and tired old roofs like lids on stunted lives.

The bus suddenly pulled up at a stop. It caught George by surprise. He could hear more people getting on. Real life was flooding back.

He could see the road now where he went scratching on the Shoprider. There was a police car parked in the middle of it with its lights flashing. George suddenly felt nervous. He spied a tube station up ahead. Perhaps it was time to get off and use a more efficient mode of transport. The situation was made worse by the woman now in front of him. She'd just got on. Yakking on her mobile phone, clamping it to her ear and smiling blankly into the middle distance. Punctuating the conversation with oooohs and aaahs and oh my Gods, as if she were cooing over a puppy.

He had to get off.

George took his bag and made his way to the top of the stairs as quickly as he could. Suddenly the bus pulled away from the stop. He staggered down the stairs as it rocked through the traffic, grabbing everything he could to stop himself from falling.

After several grumpy minutes standing by the door and glaring at the driver he finally got off the bus at the next stop. He was already feeling exhausted and couldn't help shaking his fist at a moped as it growled past, like a cow mooing at top volume through a clapped-out speaker.

The Devil was near by. He knew it. In the form of two policemen who seemed to be watching him from the other side of the road. He was determined not to be afraid of demons and devils, with their clanking moves and flea blows, but he would leave them to their business none the less and head straight for the tube.

He got through the ticket barrier with Clarissa's pass and parked himself on an escalator. Anything was better than the corkscrew stairs. There was a busker at the bottom playing an ancient guitar. He looked defeated and old before his time, dressed up in a dirty winter coat despite the season. He was bald, except for two tufts of grey hair above his temples. In front of him was a small pool of coins in a paper cup. Mostly coppers.

The busker stopped playing for a moment as George approached.

'I want you to have these,' said George, rummaging around in his bag and giving him the coins from Clarissa's white envelope. 'They're old, but they might still be worth something.'

'Aren't we all,' said the busker, thanking George as he dropped them into the paper cup. 'It's much appreciated, guv. This next song's for you . . .'

George could hear the song as he stood on the sparsely populated platform, staring across the rails at the damp-patch maps of other worlds and the big-stain faces of the harpies hidden in the peeling walls.

'Somewheeeeeere ooooover the rainbow', sang the busker, 'blooooobiiiiirds fly.'

George was definitely over the rainbow now, and he knew it.

He was heading for Thade Street and a brand-new start. He could hardly wait. 'If happy little bluebirds fly beyond the rainbow,' he said to himself, 'then why, oh why can't I?'

He looked towards the tunnel. It was like a black hole. A man was pacing up and down like a nervous dog at the end of the platform, running his hand across his hairless head in an obsolete gesture that had obviously once been comforting. Behind him there was a woman in a red cardigan, sitting on a bench nursing a suitcase on wheels.

There were distant rumblings now from the darkness of the tunnel as the cattle train approached, before it suddenly thundered into the station, all fleeting windows and screaming brakes. The woman with the suitcase stood up and readied herself for the scrum, while the pacing man just kept on pacing.

The carriage looked crowded as the doors sighed open. George stepped inside, clutching his bag as he jostled briefly with the frowning hordes before somehow managing to find a seat. As the train pulled away, with the empty platform flitting by like a life coming to an end, he could see the pacing man still pacing. Perhaps that's all he ever did.

George closed his eyes as the train screeched through the darkness of the tunnels. When he opened them again the woman opposite was staring at him. She was fat, and her big arms jutted from her gaudy blue blouse as if they'd recently sprouted from her armpits. Her hair was the colour of ashes, and her face was stark and heavy with make-up. All greased red lips and sepia teeth, with rock-hard eyes that looked as if they were about to reach out and grab him with tiny glistening hands. He knew those eyes.

He tried to look away, in desperation studying the vacuous

advertisements posted above all the passengers with their scowling faces, like bigots filled with tiny wars. But to no avail. The woman was still staring at him. There she blazed with shoulders hunched, grinding her teeth as if recalling a grudge, one of hundreds filed and graded.

At last, the robot voice announced over the Tannoy that the next stop was approaching.

George watched as the fat woman readied herself, suddenly leaning forward in her seat, then rocking back and sinking for a moment before finally heaving herself up as the train pulled into the station. She pitched forward slightly as she walked, as if carrying a heavy weight upon her back. The doors slid open, and George sighed with relief as she stepped slowly from the carriage. For a while she stood and stared at him through the window with her face becoming more and more vivid. He was sure he could see white smoke gathering around her as the train closed its doors.

As the train pulled away from the station George caught sight of the woman in the red cardigan wheeling the suitcase. She was making her way swiftly towards the exit. The train was following her now as it edged along the platform, and the woman was waving as she walked, smiling as she went.

She turned to look at George. Tears filled his eyes when he saw her face.

It was Clarissa.

19

MOON RIVER

George got off the train at the next stop. He couldn't wait to see the outside world again, a desire made even greater by traipsing through the tiled tunnels and climbing the bleak stone steps. It was early evening now, and the station was busy, which made everything even slower, including the already sluggish escalators. Soon he would be free to tread the dull cracked pavements criss-crossed by the herd, free to mingle with the crowd and drift like the vagabond poor, roaming the overripe streets like a child lost on a moor.

His enthusiasm was already beginning to wane.

The sky was turning blue as he crossed the road and made his way slowly towards the bridge. He was starting to feel uneasy, and for a while he stood beside the railings staring down at the shabby stone-bound beach. He closed his eyes and took a deep breath. It would be hard to cross the bridge, but he had no choice. It was time to move on. Time to get over the Thames and get back to Thade Street.

The tide was out, and as he watched the grey-green water spill on to the bank the memories came flooding back. He could feel the water heaving all around him, trying to drag him down into the depths. Sinking then surfacing again, each noisome struggle punctuated by a sudden all-engulfing silence as he plunged back down with the ice-cold darkness pressed against his ears.

He could hear the sirens and smell the river's sly unholy stench as he climbed the steps up to the bridge. All he could think about was being dragged from the water by the woman with the stony eyes and the moon behind her head. He could see those eyes glistening now in the metal grid beneath his feet as he walked.

When he was about halfway across the bridge he stopped and rummaged around in his bag for the red-striped trainers that Perry had given him. After one last look he threw them over the railings into the river. He then looked down at his feet and stamped on the grid, screwing his shoe into the spot where the stony eyes had been, as if extinguishing a cigarette. There were voices all around him now as people passed. They seemed happy, and he would follow them to the other side. From here on he would stop looking down and try to look ahead.

As he neared the end of the bridge he could see a man begging. He was dressed as a clown, with a big Tudor ruff and a red-spotted jumpsuit. As George approached he could hear him asking passers-by for change in a small and piteous voice. 'Please have mercy upon a poor blind clown,' he was saying, pointing a thin white stick at a hat full of coins. His face was snow white with two big tufts of scarlet hair above his temples, and he was wearing blacked-out glasses that rested on his cherry nose. When he spoke his yellow teeth flashed between his painted lips.

George stopped and looked at the coins in the upended hat. He bent down and picked one of them up. It was old currency, no longer valid. The other coins were the same, like the ones he'd given the busker from Clarissa's envelope. 'Where did you get these?' he asked.

'People give them to me,' said the clown. 'But I'm blind, so I can't see what they give me.'

George continued sifting through the coins. He looked at the clown. The lines around his mouth were deepening, and his chin was starting to protrude. 'Leave my money alone,' said the clown, poking his stick aggressively at the hat.

'But these coins are not legal tender.'

'Well, I'm sure there are lots of antique shops that might give me something for them,' said the clown, now kneeling and waving his stick randomly in the air. 'Can somebody help me?' he suddenly shouted. 'This man is a thief!'

George could see a policeman approaching, talking to his radio as he made his way along the bridge. He slowly stood up.

'Stop, thief!' yelled the clown, still waving his stick.

'I was simply saying that these coins aren't legal tender,' said George as the policeman approached.

'Please, sir, put the stick down and stop your noise,' said the policeman with his walkie-talkie blaring.

'But he was stealing my money,' said the clown, sitting back down and laying his stick down beside him.

'What's in the bag, sir?' said the policeman.

'I was just telling him that someone has given him invalid currency,' said George, letting the policeman rifle through the bag.

He was now desperate to get off the bridge. He could see the river shifting beneath him, its surface jagged in the worsening wind like a crocodile's back. After a few minutes he was allowed to leave. He knew he was being watched as he made his way down the stone steps. He hated stairs at the best of times and loathed them with a passion at the worst.

From the riverbank he made his way up to the high street,

looking back every few paces to check that he wasn't being followed. On the corner of the street was a pub. It was almost dusk now, and the weak-kneed clientele was already spilling out on to the pavement, slapping each other's backs and miming violence between gulps of beer. As he passed the decorative-glass doorway he could see the fervent faces inside, feuding with the tables and the shabby velveteen seats. Someone looked at him and raised his glass.

George moved on as quickly as he could.

The trees were shifting in the wind now as he walked, and the sky was turning grey again. He thought about Clarissa wheeling her suitcase. Perhaps he would see her . . . He should have asked her where she was going.

It was summer, but the leaves were already falling. They were spread along the pavement with the discarded coffee cups and empty beer cans, all blowing in the wind behind him. It sounded as if he was being followed, and he kept looking around to check. Which was why he didn't see the clown waiting around the bend, hiding in the doorway, ready to trip him up with his white stick.

George fell full-length on to the ground as he stumbled over the stick. He lay there for a moment amid the leaves, analysing the damage and clutching his bag, breathless with shock. Slowly, he rolled on to his back. The clown was standing over him now in his red-spotted jumpsuit. He looked down at George and slowly removed his blacked-out glasses with the cherry nose attached.

'Look. I'm healed,' he said. 'I can see you. Luck of the Devil, eh?'

George could see his lily-white face now exposed. His eyes were black as coals, and his nose was pointed, almost beak-like.

He sucked on the limp cigarette between his leather lips and stared down at George, with the smoke gathering in his head like some big bogus thought.

'You're a bloody liar,' said George, attempting to get up.

'Please try not to move,' said the clown, with smoke now billowing from his nostrils like a dragon whose sparkplugs had failed.

Suddenly George lunged at the clown's midriff, pushing him backwards with all his might so that his coccyx hit the pavement with full force. The clown flinched and screamed out in pain. There was agony on his face. 'Help me,' he cried, waving his white stick. 'I can't move . . . Help, police!'

George walked away as quickly as he could, heading for the underpass that would take him to Thade Street.

'I'll be back,' shouted the clown behind him, still lying on the ground among the leaves. 'This is only the beginning.'

It was getting dark now, and George could hear the traffic thundering overhead as he entered the underpass. It was lit by a sparse row of fluorescent lamps, which highlighted the elaborate graffiti on the tiled walls. He was walking towards the light at the other end of the tunnel as quickly as he could, with his steps echoing around him, instinctively clutching his bag even more tightly than before. Nothing would stop him getting to Thade Street. Not even the figure that was now standing ahead. A silhouette wearing a baggy jumpsuit, blocking the light and brandishing a stick.

'I told you I'd be back,' called out the clown, his voice echoing down the walls. 'And this time I've brought some friends.'

Suddenly the lights went out. He could hear voices all around him. No words, just grunts and stunted screams. Soon he could see shadows streaming into the tunnel. They were swarming around him like hellhounds. Engulfing him, tugging at his clothes, trying to drag him down into the darkness.

He was struggling to stay afloat.

He could see the clown advancing with his stick, which had now become a truncheon. His whitewashed face seemed to glow in the gloom, and his dark reptilian eyes were glinting like jet. Suddenly, he rushed at George with his baton raised. George ducked. Dropping his bag, he grabbed the baton from the clown and struck him hard across the face. He fell backwards, and there was a ghastly cracking sound, like a coconut splitting, as his head hit the concrete. The shadows swiftly shrank away, and the tunnel's scanty lights slowly flickered back to life one by one.

George was shaking now as he picked up his bag. He could see the blood spilling from the clown's head. It was like ink leaking on to the pale stone. There was no time to waste. He took a deep breath, left the tunnel and began climbing the steps up to the street.

He stopped for a moment halfway up. He was still shaking.

'Don't panic,' said a voice at the top of the stairs.

It was Perry. He was looking down at the clown's prostrate body. George looked, too. But the body had changed. Perhaps it was the distance, but it now looked like a young boy, curled up and lifeless on the cold stone floor.

'Here's looking at you, kid,' said Perry, suddenly close by.

George could feel tears flooding his eyes. He looked around, but Perry had gone.

It was time to move on again. He was almost there.

The memories were flooding back now as he left the main road and headed for the side-streets. As a boy he'd always thought the world was hollow and that the stars were cities. There was such a lot of world to see, and every night he'd look up at the resplendent cities as they glistened above the pointed roofs. After his father died and he moved to Thade Street with his mother, he imagined that if someone was looking down from one of the cities they'd see that a small part of London had gone dark for ever.

The streetlamps were on now as he turned the corner into Thade Street, and he could already see faces at misted windows, smudged like charcoal drawings. For the last few minutes he'd been followed by a brown dog, like an escort, guiding him and guarding him at the same time. Now that he was close to the house it was sitting down on the pavement, as if it couldn't come any closer. George looked at the dog. It seemed eager to play, but when he slapped his thigh in a welcoming gesture it was reluctant to advance. It then got up and walked the other way.

He stood outside the front door, suddenly feeling nervous. He felt tired, too. His violent outbursts in the tunnel had left his musculoskeletal system aching, not to mention the effect on his nerves, and he was keen to rest. As he stood there fishing in his bag for the key he started whispering to himself. 'There's no place like home . . . There's no place like home . . .'

At last he found the key and tried it in the lock. It didn't fit. He could feel his heart thumping. It wouldn't even go in, let alone turn. Why, for God's sake? He was beginning to panic.

'Judy, my love,' he said, closing his eyes. 'Please help me stay calm.'

He took a deep breath and tried a different key. The door clicked open with ease, and he stepped into the hall. He tried the light switch, but it didn't work. Suddenly, in the darkness, he was overwhelmed by memories.

He could hear noises coming from the rooms in league with the shadows. Bumps and thumps and little creaks. He stood there for a moment not sure whether he should stay or leave. He was feeling tired. Where was the handrail when you needed it? He tried the light switch again. Nothing. For now, he'd have to be thankful for the fitful glare of the streetlamp.

Suddenly the front door slammed behind him. He heard somebody cough. One of those strange suppressed coughs that sound like a spade repeatedly digging into hard soil. Then the clank of a cup and saucer. The sound was coming from the front room.

George began inching his way up the hall towards the doorway.

He peered through the crack in the door. It was in darkness, except for the light from the streetlamp, which was falling on the painting of the palm tree above the fireplace. He could see the brown carpet and the off-white walls, the velvet curtains with the dusty pelmet and the grey embroidered nets at the windows. He spied a solid-looking woman wearing a headscarf, sitting in the corner and drinking from a teacup. She looked towards the door and raised her cup as if in salutation. She then put down the cup and, to George's horror, slowly stood up. She looked as if she was in pain as she made her way to the door, with her big feet scraping across the thin carpet and her elbows stuck out like wing stumps.

George could see her face now. It seemed to be deteriorating the closer it came. Her jaw was jutting to one side, with two teeth protruding over her bottom lip. There was a cushion of saliva where they rested. One of her eyes was missing. The socket had skinned over, and the pupil of the remaining eye was looking skywards.

She neared the crack then disappeared for a moment, before poking her hideous head out at him. Something like a smile passed across her lipless mouth, which was now moving as if she was trying to speak. George looked at her in horror.

'Get out of here,' she said in a broken voice. 'I don't care how troubled you are.' She pointed to the front door. 'Bang bang . . . THUMP,' she whispered.

George could hear a key being inserted into the lock at the front door.

He had no choice but to make his way upstairs as quickly as he could. He could smell burning as he gripped the balustrade – although it wasn't so much fire as the thick black scent of burnt-out rooms. He closed his eyes for a moment and tried to calm himself.

'Judy,' he said aloud. 'Oh, please be there.'

When he finally reached the landing he could see that the door was ajar. 'It's me,' he said quietly as he made his way over to the bed. 'I'm back, Judy. I'm sorry it took so long. I think I remembered everything . . .'

For a while he stood there in the half-light, staring down at the empty bed with the clock ticking relentlessly. 'Where did you go?' he whispered. There were tears in his eyes.

He could hear noises downstairs now. He slumped to his knees and put his hand beneath the bed. Slowly he pulled out a wooden box. He then removed the lid and took out the contents. He put his coat on the bed and slipped the yellow satin tunic over his shirt. It was cold to the touch, and its brass buttons glinted in the light from the streetlamp. Next he took off his flares and brown loafers and donned the red silken trousers and fur-lined boots. Finally he reached beneath the bed again and pulled out a walking-stick, which he hid carefully in the corner next to his bag. It was thick and looked like a pike, and it would finish anyone who dared to come upstairs.

He felt tired now. He pulled the curtains. The scraping sound was a little louder than he'd anticipated, and the room was suddenly pitch-dark. He walked over to the high-backed chair and sat down, clutching the last item in the wooden clothes box. It was a striped silken cap with a bell on top, and it pinged as he placed it on the chair arm.

'Good night, Judy. My Huckleberry friend.' He slowly closed his eyes. 'Sweet dreams, my darling girl,' he said, wondering whether he ought to have his walking-stick to hand . . .

Within moments he was asleep.

Drawing found in Room 22,
Bayview Retirement Home

'Home Sweet Home', dated 2014

20

WELCOME HOME

George's eyes were closed, but he could sense people all around him. When he finally opened them all he could see was the ceiling. He was lying in bed, barely able to move. Suddenly he heard the scrape of a curtain rail. A scrawny man wearing a white coat was beside him now, staring down at him with stony eyes.

'You're very lucky to be here, you know,' said the man, smiling and clutching a clipboard. 'I do hope we've made you feel welcome.'

George blinked the sleep away and scowled. He could feel a thick white plaster collar locked around his neck. What had they done to him?

'You must be glad to see me,' said the man, his smile now more of a sneer. 'Please try not to move. My name is Dr Mara. Do you remember yours?'

George looked up at the man's bony face with its sharp, almost beak-like nose. He made the shape of a crucifix with his fingers. '*In nomine Patris et Filii et Spiritus Sancti*,' he said, trying to lift his hand up to the man's face.

Mara smiled and waved his hand in front of his face as if swatting a fly. 'And the same to you.'

'My name is Mr Punch,' said George. It was the first name that came into his head.

Mara stood up stiffly, took a pen from his breast pocket and wrote something on his clipboard. 'May I have a chair, please?' he asked loudly.

He heard the sound of the scraping rail again. The blue nylon curtains that surrounded the bed suddenly opened with a swish, and a young man appeared. He placed a metal chair beside the bed and smiled briefly at George. 'My name's Jack,' he said. 'Nice to meet you.' He closed the curtains as swiftly as he'd opened them.

Dr Mara sat down on the chair beside George. 'What the devil happened to you?' he asked, pointing the pen at George as if it were a stick. 'Did somebody try to hurt you? You've been badly injured, you know.'

'Why, doctor,' said George, eyeing the liver spots on Mara's bald pate. 'I do believe you've lost all your hair.'

Mara briefly groomed the feathery patches at his temples and tried another smile. 'I think you need some physic for your injuries,' he said.

George frowned. 'I know who you are,' he said. 'Or, rather, what you are. And you're certainly no doctor.'

Mara stood up and scratched more words on to his clipboard. Just then the curtains scraped open again and a portly woman in a white coat stepped forward.

'Come on in,' said Mara, addressing the woman. He pointed down at George. 'I suppose some kind of trauma was inevitable with an injury of this kind. As well as some damage to the vocal folds.'

'Hence the inhibition of vocal-tract resonance,' said the woman.

Mara nodded sagely. 'Yes. And the extensive use of the nasal cavity as an articulator.' He tapped the clipboard with his pen.

'He's bound to be delirious for a while. And there will, of course, be some memory loss.'

George tried to move his legs. He was shocked at how weak he was. He managed to turn his head a little, but all he could see now were big grey machines on portable tables.

'Please try not to move,' said Dr Mara a little irritably. 'You'll only make things worse.'

'He must be very tired after his ordeal,' said the woman. 'Maybe we should give him some time to recoup. And perhaps a little something to help him along . . .'

'I don't like taking physic,' said George. 'It gives me a headache.'

'That's because you don't take enough of it,' said the portly woman, staring down at him. Her face looked pale, with thin scarlet lips and vivid eyes. 'You nearly died, remember? You're lucky to be alive . . .'

George looked up at her stony eyes. 'Am I in Heaven yet?' he asked.

There was a light behind her head. It made her look as if she had a halo. 'Not if we can help it.'

He closed his eyes for a moment then looked up at the ceiling with its built-in sixty-watt halogen lights. He was beginning to feel cold. He could feel the freezing river all around him, its beaten surface rising and falling like a creature deep in slumber. He was struggling for breath now as it sucked him down, down into the depths . . .

He woke with a start. He rubbed his eyes and peered into the gloom. All he could see now was the crude sketch of a room. Sideboard, bed, bookshelves, chairs, the usual roll-call required for so-called civilized living.

It was dawn, and he could hear the birds were singing. He

stood up and donned his striped silken cap, proud of its jingling bell. He was feeling more sprightly than he had done for a very long time. The room seemed to be getting brighter by the minute. He could see the sunlight burning the edges of the curtains. He could even see the photographs on the side-board. He'd only ever recognized one of them. It was his wedding day. There he was, done up to the nines, beside his beloved Judy in her green embroidered dress, with the happy couple flanked by their bridesmaids – or should that be brides-dogs? – Burt and Hal.

There was a sudden noise in the hall. It sounded like the slamming of a door.

George quickly grabbed his walking-stick, which he'd left in the corner of the room the night before. He then snapped it over his knee and attempted an arthritic little dance – he wasn't going to be dragged down any more.

There was another noise. More of a thump this time. Some-one or something was making its way upstairs, slowly and deliberately, trying not to make any noise.

His thin red silken trousers made a swishing sound as he walked over to the sideboard. The padded yellow envelope that Serena had given him was still sitting there unopened. He picked up the wedding photograph and studied it for a moment.

'Do you take this man?' he said, smiling down at Judy.

Her little face smiled back at him from the picture. 'I do,' she said.

He looked at the picture with tears in his eyes.

'Can you hear the singing?' said Judy.

'Yes, I certainly can.'

'They're calling you.' Judy smiled.

He put his face close to the picture. 'I know,' he whispered. 'I've been gone too long.'

Suddenly there was a loud knock at the door.

'Hello,' said a voice from the hall. 'Is there anybody there?'

It was followed by a succession of knocks, each one louder than the last, then the sound of a key being inserted into the lock.

George placed the photograph frame carefully back on to the sideboard and walked over to the window. He could hear the door opening. With a sudden sweeping gesture he pulled back the curtains and bowed to the world. 'Mid pleasures and palaces though we may roam, be it ever so humble, there's no place like home!'

A figure was now slowly backing into the room. It was Serena.

'Ta-da!' she said, wheeling in a food trolley. 'I've got something special for you, Mr P. It's courtesy of Bernard. He's letting everyone sample his courgettes and tomatoes. I've cooked them with butter, so they should taste delicious.'

She made her way to the window, where she paused for a moment.

'Time to rise and shine, Mr P.'

The room was silent.

'George . . . ?'

Reluctantly she walked over to the bed. She looked down at the body lying there.

It was George. He was fully clothed in an old grey coat. The trademark trainers had been replaced by featureless brown loafers, and there was a bag beside him. He looked as if he'd been about to go somewhere.

Serena took his hand. It felt cold. As she closed her eyes tears began to fall. She'd seen many deaths in her time, but this one hit her hard.

After a while she went back over to the window. It was a sunny day, but as she looked out at the blue sky it was as if part of it had suddenly gone grey.

As usual she used activity to fend off sadness. She wiped her eyes and looked around the room for something to do. Spying a wooden box beneath the bed, she knelt down and carefully slid it out on to the carpet. She removed the lid. Inside it was a pair of soft boots and some brightly coloured silken clothes, all neatly folded.

As she slid the box back under the bed there was something blocking the way. It was an old brown briefcase covered in dust. It obviously hadn't been opened for a while. Inside she found some drawings, all signed by George. Smudged portraits, some of them disfigured, others merely old. George had always said that he liked drawing, but she'd never seen any evidence of it. Along with the drawings there was an envelope of old photographs, all of them black and white. One of them was of a small boy in a blue jumper holding George's hand. They were both smiling.

Serena took a deep breath and closed her eyes. Tears were running down her face now as she carefully put everything back inside the briefcase and slid it under the bed.

As she was preparing to leave the room she spotted the yellow envelope she'd given George. It was sitting behind the framed photos on the sideboard, still unopened.

'George,' she whispered tearfully as she held it in her hand. 'Why didn't you open the package I gave you?'

She took a deep breath and opened the envelope.

Gradually the vivid face of a puppet inched its way out of

the package. It was attached to a withered cloth body with the words 'REMEMBER ME?' written on a piece of card around its neck. It was Mr Punch. A glove puppet. A cartoon. A caricature with a lantern jaw and a sturdy conk of a nose. Serena couldn't help but smile as she held its wraith-like body in her hand, despite its lurid features.

After a few moments she reluctantly placed the puppet back on the sideboard, propping it up behind the photos. She'd been slowly trying to reintroduce George to his past, but it hadn't worked. In fact, the packages had only made it worse.

She looked tearfully at the photos, lined up like dusty windows on to better times. The biggest of them featured two faces poking out from a cartoon picture board of Punch and Judy wearing colourful wedding outfits and flanked by two dogs dressed as bridesmaids. It had obviously been taken by the seaside.

Beside it was another photograph. Black and white. Very different. It was of a handsome young George standing beside a Punch and Judy booth. He had a puppet on each hand, and he was smiling for the camera.

'That's the way to do it,' said Serena. It was the only Punch and Judy phrase she knew.

The other photograph was in colour, but it had faded in the sunlight and now had a faint yellow tinge. It was a close-up of George's Punch and Judy booth, festooned with a painting of Mr Punch, presumably done by George. Below it there was a picture of a small boy, with the words: 'In memory of Tom, who will always be with us.'

Serena took a deep breath and went over to the window. Sunny skies were what she needed now. In the sunlight she could see a mark on the glass just above the sill. She pulled the net curtain back. There was a small handprint in the corner of the window.

As she stared at the handprint she realized that it was time to move on.

'We'll miss you, George,' she sighed, wheeling the redundant food trolley to the door. 'But at least you're going home at last.'

21

WHAT A WONDERFUL WORLD

I can hear the birds singing sweetly now as I cross the fore-court. The trees are green again at last, and my leaden coat is gone. I feel lighter than I've ever felt before. The red roses on the corner are no longer sores but gifts from Eros, and the houses near the high street are not grey after all, their gravel drives not cramped but snug.

As I look back at Bayview for the last time I can see my old friend and ex-colleague Horace, the world's second greatest Punch and Judy man. We used to turn up the radio and do silly dances for the crowd between our shows. Dressed up to the nines we were. It's what Punch and Judy men do.

He's waving from the window now, and I'm waving back.

'*Bonŝancon*, George,' he yells. It means good luck in Esper-anto. It was all the rage back in the 1960s.

'*Ĝis baldaŭ*,' I yell back. That's 'See you soon.'

I'm heading for the park. The high street is busy as usual, but the sun is shining and the sky is blue, and everything seems so much clearer. There's the Bartholomew Arms and Edmunds Cut Price Store (apostrophe not needed – it's a name after all).

I can see Upton Silver getting out of his van. He's shivering and a-shaking and waving like a loon. I'm returning the compliment and waving back. He used to perform with us in Brighton in the 1970s, crooning at the end of the pier. We had some great times with Upton, especially when he ended up giving us a lift back home.

'You're Always on My Mind,' I shout.

'And You'll Never Walk Alone,' he shouts back, waving.

As I cross the road I can see Perry on the traffic island wearing his famous red-striped Nike trainers.

'Didn't he do well?' he says as I approach. 'I'm just off over the road.'

'Well, do be careful,' I tell him. 'You know what happened last time.'

'Frankly, my dear, I don't give a damn,' he says as we amble across the road together. 'Go ahead,' he says, gesturing at the speeding cars. 'Make my day.'

He's leading me to a café with its tables under a canopy. 'You know, I've never liked pubs, Georgie,' he says.

It was Perry who was out drinking with my father that fateful night when the bomb exploded at the Railway Tavern. The irony was that they'd both survived the war together. Perry was injured in the blast but only partially. He ended up losing one of his fingers. He'd tried to save a small boy as he crawled from the site, but the boy had died. He was almost a father figure, and he stayed friends with Mum and me right up until his death in a road accident in the late 1980s.

He said he'd never forgotten the little boy.

As Perry and I approach the café I spy Tom beneath one of the tables. He's always been mischievous and sometimes a little too brave for his own good.

'Here's looking at you, kid,' says Perry, bending down to look under the table.

'You were right, pops,' says Tom, climbing out and grabbing my hand.

'About what?' I ask.

'That boy in Perry's room,' says Tom. 'I told him he could walk out of the place whenever he wanted. And he did. We're best friends now.' Tom points to some chairs near by where the little boy is hiding. He pokes his head out and waves.

'Guess where I'm going now,' he continues excitedly. He runs over to one of the tables. I can see my mother and father sitting there. Mum is pouring the tea, with steam rising from the cup. Dad waves at me as Tom gives him a hug.

'Thank you for freeing the boy,' says Perry, looking me in the face and firmly shaking my hand. 'He'd always been near by, ever since that dark sacred night. He needed to be released. And now, so do you.'

'I know,' I say, smiling. 'But don't panic. I'll be back.'

I look at Dad. 'Bon happy tea!' he says, holding his cup aloft and giving me the thumbs-up. 'See you very soon, Georgie.'

I carry on up the high street. I can see Perry saluting behind me. As I turn around and return the gesture, I catch sight of myself in a shop window with my steel-grey hair and slender nose. I'd always wished my nose was bigger and more memorable, like that of Mr Punch. But at least I don't have his stoop.

Over the road I can see my bookworm cousin, Bernard. I suppose, in a way, I've always been envious of him. I didn't try hard enough at school, and he always made me feel inferior. He's sitting on a bench now outside the bookshop, reading the papers. Probably the broadsheets, as per usual. He's waving at me and pointing to the books beside him on the bench. I give him the thumbs-up and wave back. There's a dog at his feet. It lifts its head as if to say hello, and I can't help smiling.

In fact, I can feel a sense of overwhelming joy now as I walk. What was once an apoplectic shuffle has once again become a sprightly step.

Suddenly I begin to dance along the pavement. I am overjoyed. This is a bright, blessed day, and I should be thankful for it.

I can see my beloved Clarissa now. She's smiling, and in a moment we're dancing together in the sunlight. Waltzing on the pavement. I've never been happier. It's all a long way from that dark and dreadful night when she fell down the stairs. Bang bang . . . THUMP.

'From now on', I say, with my arms around her, 'I will never cower. I'll blossom and I'll bloom and I'll burst right into flower.'

'We both will,' she says. 'I promise.'

Clarissa has always been there, ever since my first Punch and Judy performance when she went around the crowd collecting money in a paper cup after the show. We kept those coins in an envelope, and we never let them go.

'Can you hear the singing?' she asks as we dance.

I put my face close to hers. 'Yes, my love, I can.'

'They're calling you, George,' she whispers. 'You must go now. But please come back very soon.'

'Just try stopping me,' I say.

I can see Tom now, running towards us from the café. He runs headlong into his mother and gives her a hug.

'Don't I get one, too, Tom?' I say.

'No, Dad. You get three!' says Tom, putting his arms around me three times.

He seems filled with the joys of life, more than I ever was.

'Mum,' he says, looking up at Clarissa, slightly breathless. 'Where's pops going?'

'He's going home,' she says, taking Tom's hand. 'But then he's coming back again to see us and will stay with us for ever.'

Everything looks vivid as I make my way towards the park with its grand gateway. This side of the rainbow all the colours seem brighter, and I can already smell the flowers.

As I look back I can see all the people from all the moments, young and old, stopping in their tracks and waving me goodbye. Friends shaking hands, saluting me, wishing me good luck, *bon voyage*, *au revoir*, God go with you, been nice knowing you, bon happy tea . . .

And I think to myself, what a wonderful world.

Photograph found in Room 22,
Bayview Retirement Home

SOME AUTHORS WE HAVE PUBLISHED

James Agee • Bella Akhmadulina • Tariq Ali • Kenneth Allsop • Alfred Andersch
Guillaume Apollinaire • Machado de Assis • Miguel Angel Asturias • Duke of Bedford
Oliver Bernard • Thomas Blackburn • Jane Bowles • Paul Bowles • Richard Bradford
Ilse, Countess von Bredow • Lenny Bruce • Finn Carling • Blaise Cendrars • Marc Chagall
Giorgio de Chirico • Uno Chiyo • Hugo Claus • Jean Cocteau • Albert Cohen
Colette • Ithell Colquhoun • Richard Corson • Benedetto Croce • Margaret Crosland
e.e. cummings • Stig Dalager • Salvador Dali • Osamu Dazai • Anita Desai
Charles Dickens • Bernard Diederich • Fabián Dobles • William Donaldson
Autran Dourado • Yuri Druzhnikov • Lawrence Durrell • Isabelle Eberhardt
Sergei Eisenstein • Shusaku Endo • Erté • Knut Faldbakken • Ida Fink
Wolfgang George Fischer • Nicholas Freeling • Philip Freund • Carlo Emilio Gadda
Rhea Galanaki • Salvador Garmendia • Michel Gauquelin • André Gide
Natalia Ginzburg • Jean Giono • Geoffrey Gorer • William Goyen • Julien Gracq
Sue Grafton • Robert Graves • Angela Green • Julien Green • George Grosz
Barbara Hardy • H.D. • Rayner Heppenstall • David Herbert • Gustaw Herling
Hermann Hesse • Shere Hite • Stewart Home • Abdullah Hussein • King Hussein of Jordan
Ruth Inglis • Grace Ingoldby • Yasushi Inoue • Hans Henny Jahnn • Karl Jaspers
Takeshi Kaiko • Jaan Kaplinski • Anna Kavan • Yasunuri Kawabata • Nikos Kazantzakis
Orhan Kemal • Christer Kihlman • James Kirkup • Paul Klee • James Laughlin
Patricia Laurent • Violette Leduc • Lee Seung-U • Vernon Lee • József Lengyel
Robert Liddell • Francisco García Lorca • Moura Lympany • Thomas Mann
Dacia Maraini • Marcel Marceau • André Maurois • Henri Michaux • Henry Miller
Miranda Miller • Marga Minco • Yukio Mishima • Quim Monzó • Margaret Morris
Angus Wolfe Murray • Atle Næss • Gérard de Nerval • Anaïs Nin • Yoko Ono
Uri Orlev • Wendy Owen • Arto Paasilinna • Marco Pallis • Oscar Parland
Boris Pasternak • Cesare Pavese • Milorad Pavic • Octavio Paz • Mervyn Peake
Carlos Pedretti • Dame Margery Perham • Graciliano Ramos • Jeremy Reed
Rodrigo Rey Rosa • Joseph Roth • Ken Russell • Marquis de Sade • Cora Sandel
Iván Sándor • George Santayana • May Sarton • Jean-Paul Sartre
Ferdinand de Saussure • Gerald Scarfe • Albert Schweitzer
George Bernard Shaw • Isaac Bashevis Singer • Patwant Singh • Edith Sitwell
Suzanne St Albans • Stevie Smith • C.P. Snow • Bengt Söderbergh
Vladimir Soloukhin • Natsume Soseki • Muriel Spark • Gertrude Stein • Bram Stoker
August Strindberg • Rabindranath Tagore • Tambimuttu • Elisabeth Russell Taylor
Emma Tennant • Anne Tibble • Roland Topor • Miloš Urban • Anne Valery
Peter Vansittart • José J. Veiga • Tarjei Vesaas • Noel Virtue • Max Weber
Edith Wharton • William Carlos Williams • Phyllis Willmott
G. Peter Winnington • Monique Wittig • A.B. Yehoshua • Marguerite Young
Fakhar Zaman • Alexander Zinoviev • Emile Zola

 Peter Owen Publishers, 81 Ridge Road, London N8 9NP, UK
T + 44 (0)20 8350 1775 / E info@peterowen.com
www.peterowen.com / @PeterOwenPubs
Independent publishers since 1951